Praise for Steve Dancy Tales

"The James Best books ... are about the best new western series to come along since Larry McMurtry."

True West Magazine

"You'll find yourself lost in the book—the fast pace keeps it interesting."

Maritza Barone, *Woman's Day*

"James D. Best the author has written at least six books, including the Steve Dancy Western novels. I read them and enjoyed them immensely."

Gary Clothier, *Star Democrat*

"This is a fast-paced tale with an interesting hero ... you'll certainly find enough twists and turns to provide an entertaining and exciting story."

Western Writers of America

"A lively, old-fashioned style Western—clever, entertaining, and full of period references to give it authenticity. Best paces his stories so well readers will find it difficult to put down."

Diane Scearce, *Nashville Examiner*

"A great book; I do hope that *The Shopkeeper* gets the readership it richly deserves."

Simon Barrett, Blogger News Network

"Once again, Best has penned a fine read."

Roundup Magazine

"I loved it! The story is told in such a classic, smooth tone—it's really fast paced throughout."

Jonathon Lyons, Lyons Literary

"James D. Best is arguably one of the best writers of westerns."

Alan Caruba, *Bookviews*

"I would highly recommend these westerns to anyone with an imagination and curiosity about the history of our country. And besides, they are just excellent reading."

Holgerson's Book and Bookstore

"This is a compelling narrative and as good as the best of classic westerns. James D. Best is a name to remember."

Saline River Chronicle

"The writing is clear and straightforward with plenty of action attached. For an entertaining read, *The Shopkeeper* draws high marks."

T. Akery, *'Bout Books*

"Great stories, interesting and diverse characters and plenty of action! I have enjoyed every one of them. I can't wait for the next one and hope it comes soon!"

Larry Winget, The Pitbull of Personal Development

"James D. Best is one of my new favorite authors. I highly recommend this well-written and entertaining series!"

Glorianne Muggli at *Miligero*

"This sequel to the author's Steve Dancy series is as good as they come."

Roundup Magazine

"…even if I weren't living in Leadville, I'd still love this Wild West mystery adventure! Best's writing style is a romp, and he nails the dialogue. Two thumbs up!"

Leadville Laurel @ Leadville Literary League

Praise for Tempest at Dawn

"The best novel EVER on the U.S. Constitution."

Larry Schweikart, professor of history and author
A Patriot's History of the United States and a dozen other history books

"If you want to know the truth about the character of those gentlemen and you want to learn about the evolution of one of the greatest documents ever created by man---the Constitution of the United States---relax in your bed, favorite chair or recliner, and enjoy."

Allen Ball, *Beaufort Observer*

"Thanks to James Best's masterpiece, *Tempest at Dawn*, I felt like the 56th delegate at the Constitutional Convention. Using vivid narrative and expressive dialogue, *Tempest at Dawn* presents all the major issues the Founding Fathers struggled with."

Michael E. Newton, author
The Path to Tyranny, Angry Mobs and the Founding Fathers, Alexander Hamilton.

"The novel captures the real drama that ensued behind closed doors as they hammered out what is now the oldest living constitution and the foundation of the nation. Read it for its historical value. Read it for its dramatic value. But read it!"

Alan Caruba, *Bookviews*

Praise for The Shut Mouth Society

"*The Shut Mouth Society* is a fast-moving, well-written novel."

David M. Kinchen, *Huntington News*

"The author has done an excellent job of building the story. I wanted to know more about the secret societies, more about the Sherman family, and more about the resolution."

Book Advice

"The Shut Mouth Society by James D. Best is the kind of book I like best. The novel has everything from intrigue and murder to romance."

Faith Friese Nelson, *A Writer's Journal*

No Peace

James D. Best

A Steve Dancy Tale

Also by James D. Best

For Mike Cunningham
I miss him.

Regret lasts longer than guilt.
Barbara Cunningham ©

Chapter 1

"Eight."

William Adams pronounced the number with a barely concealed smirk. I didn't like the man. His boast to have thrown eight strikeouts for Harvard against my alma mater irked me. Harvard men took pleasure in disparaging lesser schools, which they thought included all other institutions of higher learning. Damn, I wished my mother had never mentioned my degree from Columbia. I could tell from William's demeanor that he thought school rivalry would be a dandy subject for breakfast conversation. I wasn't going to have any of it.

I ignored his taunt and asked, "Mother, are your accommodations comfortable?"

We had met my mother and the Adamses at the Hotel Del Monte in Monterey, California. The vacation hotel sat on a knoll with a grand vista of the Pacific Ocean and Monterey Bay. Its grounds were expansive with various gardens, walking pathways, equestrian trails, and manicured lawns. Many of the trails and paths led through the Del Monte Forest to the craggy shoreline of Cypress Point.

"I'm pleased," she said, "and … surprised. One never knows what to expect when visiting the frontier. This is a wonderful alternative to Carson City. I enjoy bucolic towns, but only in limited doses." She made a point of looking down at my waist. "I must say, I'm pleased to see men don't strut around with guns on their hips, taking umbrage at the slightest annoyance."

I didn't mention that I carried a .38 pistol under my coat in a discreet shoulder holster. I also didn't mention that California had become a state in 1850. Thirty-five years of civility had tamed California, but I still felt underdressed when unarmed. I also knew that just outside the hotel grounds, remnants of wildness survived, unaffected by the washed and profanity-free gentry who patronized this fashionable resort overlooking the Pacific.

"Mrs. Dancy, did you walk the Arizona Garden this morning?" my wife asked, to change the subject.

"No, dear. My son promised a civilized respite from the heat of the city. Ugly plants scattered in the dirt do not appeal to me. On the other hand, the English gardens look wonderful. Perhaps we can stroll after our meal."

Virginia's expression never wavered. She always projected sociable interest in my mother's patrician views. I marveled at her fortitude. Virginia and I had been married for slightly over three years, and we had a son a little over two years old. Our joint holiday at the edge of the Pacific wasn't meant for my mother to escape a sweltering summer in New York City. I had invited her to meet her grandson, Jeffery Joseph Dancy. She had been in Europe when he was born and then busy planning the wedding of the other couple at our table. I had been surprised when she accepted the invitation instead of demanding that we travel to New York. Now I understood the real reason she had traveled west.

Last evening, Virginia and I were astonished to discover that Jenny Bolton and her new husband had accompanied my mother. William and Jenny Adams were returning to Nevada, where Jenny's ranch, mines, and other holdings made her an empress of sorts. Bringing them along on this holiday allowed my mother to show off her handiwork. She had adopted Jenny as a protégée and brought her back to New York with a promise to turn the rough-hewn hellion into a lady. Measured by Jenny's deportment and table manners, my mother had achieved her goal admirably. She had also pledged to procure an appropriate husband to sit at Jenny's side as she reigned over an empire that included most of the cattle, silver, and politicians in Nevada. Mother appeared to have succeeded here as well. She had polished a rough diamond until it shone so brightly, it had attracted a suitable beau. Her success in both endeavors didn't surprise me. No one had ever outdone either of these women in intelligence, ambition, or sheer will.

At twenty-one, Jenny was fifteen years younger than me. Since her husband had recently graduated from Harvard, I assumed that he was a few years older. Knowing my mother, I was certain his pedigree was pristine—although he was probably a third or fourth son, which required him to marry into money. But money wasn't Jenny's only asset. She remained strikingly pretty, and I assumed she remained smart as a whip. She didn't utter much beyond banalities, but I was certain Mother had taught her to disguise her intelligence. I suspected she had fooled William, but I knew better. I knew more. I wondered if Jenny had actually shed some of her rage, or if she had become more adept at keeping it under wraps. When I had known her earlier, she was married to a different man, forty years her senior. Her first husband had been the largest rancher in Nevada. When he decided to run for governor, a rival had him assassinated, unfortunately, right in front of Jenny. She took revenge by shrewdly killing the assassin in a manner that precluded prosecution.

How much did her new husband know of her history?

My own history was not without blemishes. I grew up highly privileged in New York City, but in 1879, I had run away from my patrician family to experience the Wild West. After gradually migrating westward, I eventually reached San Diego, and no longer able to ride into the sunset, I settled down. In truth, San Diego had less to do with my discarding my wanderlust than had my marriage and son. During my early years in the West, I had had some rough adventures, but the past few years had been blissfully peaceful. To a large degree, I had reverted to my citified upbringing.

San Diego combined poise, vibrancy, cultural novelty, and the best weather I had ever experienced. It was a grand place to live. The town remained difficult to reach, so I had suggested Monterey as a rendezvous. Santa Cruz could be reached by train from San Francisco, and then it was only a short ride around the bay to Monterey. I had another reason to visit this particular hotel, but my mother didn't need to know that just yet.

Both parties had arrived the prior afternoon and retired after brief salutations and a quick supper. We agreed to meet for breakfast at seven because my mother was an early riser, and she expected everyone to cater to her desires. The Hotel Del Monte was one of the finest resort hotels in the country—perhaps the world—so it stood a chance of garnering my mother's approval. So far, so good.

"Did you play baseball at Columbia?" Adams asked, to nudge the conversation back to his athletic prowess.

"No," I answered. "Sports in college didn't become popular until after I graduated. I concentrated—"

"They're all the rage now," Adams interjected. "Baseball, wrestling, football, all the manly sports. The Intercollegiate Football Association includes Columbia … it's been around for a decade, so surely you attended games."

Was the man ignorant or trying to make me feel old?

"Sorry, I graduated in '70. We played football at picnics and such, but it was different. Just a way to build an appetite."

"Great. Maybe this afternoon we can throw a ball around."

How could I divert the conversation again?

"Sorry, I need to concentrate on writing. My publisher wants a few chapters by the end of the week."

"Poppycock," my mother interjected. "I'll telegraph Mr. Benson and tell him he'll just have to wait. I will not have you holed up in your room during our holiday."

Damn. I had forgotten that Benson was both a distant relative and a friend of my mother. My second western novel had done well and had boosted sales for my first book. Now they wanted a third before public interest waned. I could put it aside for the length of this holiday, but I had no desire to become William Adams's mate. I could think of no way out, so I shrugged internally and put on a pleasant expression.

"In that case, I look forward to a little sport on the lawn."

Adams smiled broadly. "Fantastic. The women can watch us while Jeffie rolls in the grass. A boy should see his father engage in manly endeavors."

Adams confirmed once more that I had good reason to dislike him. I doubted we shared any interests. He epitomized high-society arrogance. I had moved to the frontier to live free of pretensions and class distinctions. In New York City, my mother never encountered a lowborn person—unless that person happened to be in her employ. In the West, people of all distinctions intermingled all the time. At a general store or saloon, a small dirt farmer might strike up a conversation with a bank manager or lawyer. In fact, Virginia and I had run a general store in Leadville, Colorado, that catered to all classes, including women of ill repute, Indians, and hardscrabble miners. Together, we had seen a lot and done a lot and had adventures that would probably curdle the blood of the highly proper Mr. Adams.

As if reading my mind, Adams asked, "I understand you once courted Jenny?"

I glanced at Virginia. She appeared amused, not angry.

"It would be more accurate to say that I requested permission to court Jenny." I turned my attention in Jenny's direction, wearing my best smile. "She declined."

"I did," Jenny said. "My husband had been recently assassinated, and it was far too early to entertain the idea of another suitor."

"Well, Steve, despite Jenny's rejection, it appears you did fine," Adams said with a snotty expression. "I'm sure it's difficult to find suitable women in the wilderness. Jenny's a rare gem … and a member of the emerging aristocracy of this wild country." He laughed. "She makes money producing real things instead of shuffling paper. After meeting Jenny, I discovered that someone has to produce these things we buy in stores." He laughed again to prove he meant his comments to be humorous. "I'm looking forward to seeing her holdings, as she calls them."

I glanced at my wife, who was clearly peeved. So was I. William had no cause to damn my wife with faint praise. However, a sharp retort would incite my mother's wrath, so I decided school rivalry wasn't such a poor subject for conversation after all.

"Speaking of athletic competition," I said, "I believe rowing is the oldest intercollegiate sport … going all the way back to '52. Yale did quite well in The Race this year."

Adams turned crimson. The rowing competition between Harvard and Yale had become so popular that people of breeding referred to it simply as "The Race." Harvard had dominated the contest until last year, when Yale pulled off a stunning upset. It appeared that my reference to the humiliating defeat upset our guest. Good.

"I don't row," Adams said defensively.

"Oh, I didn't know," I said. "I'm sure the results would have been different if you did."

Now everyone except Virginia looked peeved. Amused, she squeezed my hand under the table. I hadn't exactly defended her honor, but I had succeeded in scoring a hit with my return fire.

"When will you tire of San Diego?" my mother asked. Everyone seemed to want to change the subject of conversation.

I hesitated, then said carefully, "I doubt we will. San Diego presents great investment opportunities, and I'm developing business interests in the area, significant deals that will require my personal attention. We have a comfortable home on a picturesque island sheltered by a natural harbor. When train service comes later this year, you should visit."

"Can I travel in my car?"

"Of course, Mother. The Santa Fe is a first-rate railroad. I'm sure they'll accommodate private cars."

"Well then, we'll see. I do want to see Jeffie grow up, but you should also bring him to New York. You and Virginia can investigate proper schools for the boy." She looked directly at Virginia. "New York has some of the finest private schools."

Before Virginia could get herself in trouble, Adams diverted the conversation once again. "Yes, indeed, *some* of the finest. The very finest, however, are in Boston."

I relaxed and barely paid attention to the conversation. The two of them could joust. In the end, my mother won, as usual, but I'm not sure Adams knew it.

When the conversation paused, Virginia asked, "Will, are you a descendent of either John or Sam Adams?"

He puffed up. "Both, actually. I'm a direct descendent of two presidents. John Quincy was my grandfather." He laughed. "The family seldom mentions that rabble-rouser Sam Adams. He was a black sheep in the extended family, a cousin of his more accomplished kin."

Perfect. Adams bragged about his family for the remainder of the meal. As long as he pontificated about his lineage, we avoided barbed remarks that could escalate into arguments. In fact, I enjoyed the rest of my meal until Adams said something tactless to Virginia.

"You must forgive me, Virginia. All this discussion about the accomplishments of my family must seem quite foreign to you. I certainly didn't mean to make you feel out of place. I'm sure your relatives are very nice people."

Virginia bristled. "They are … although some don't use that phrase when referring to my uncle."

She didn't elaborate, and William did not interrogate further. Her uncle was Congressman William Morris, chairman of the Ways and Means Committee. My mother had obviously neglected to inform him of Virginia's background. She was a descendent of Robert Morris, and if memory served me right, John Adams had stayed in Morris's home until the White House was ready for occupancy.

This talk of family turned my attention to Jenny. She had been exceptionally quiet but seemed completely composed. Jenny's first husband had paid thirty dollars to wed her, and supposedly, her drunkard father was happy to see her gone. I doubted that my mother had advertised Jenny's sod-poor upbringing.

As if she had read my mind, Jenny said, "Will's family is very close and supportive. When they learned that my family had been killed by Indians, they nearly adopted me, even before we married." She wrapped both hands around Adams's upper arm and lay her cheek against his shoulder. "I feel like I have a family again."

I wondered what would happen when someone in Nevada spilled the beans.

Jenny suddenly popped to her feet. "Let's take that stroll."

We all rose with her.

Her pretty face and shy smile projected the image of an ingénue. "I love this place."

She twirled.

"It feels like something out of a storybook. Like the safest and most contented place on earth."

Chapter 2

The damn football hit me in my gut and doubled me over. Luckily, I held on to the ball. William was showing off his strong arm, and I had to run, switch directions, and leap to catch his spiral throws. I had played more ball than I'd admitted to at breakfast, but that had been over ten years ago, and I had been truthful when I said I'd played only at picnics and between classes. Obviously, William played serious football.

Virginia, Jenny, and my mother sat in wooden lawn chairs, ignoring us as they chatted. Jeffie teased the women by jumping from lap to lap. Even Jenny affected disappointment when he slid away to gather attention from someone else.

Despite leaping high in the air, I missed the next pass. When I threw the ball back, I tried to put it in William's arms, but he always threw it just out of my reach or so hard that it hurt to catch the damn thing. Adams relished making me look the fool. My body was sore in places I forgot existed, and I was done with him throwing cannonballs at me.

I waved in a friendly manner that I was done, tucked the ball under my arm, and walked toward the women. As I approached, I looked out to a smooth azure sea. It was a perfect day—sunny, windless, and not too hot. The grassy knoll provided a spectacular view of the coast and water. The Great Lawn, as the Del Monte preferred to call it, extending across the resort frontage and gently sloping toward the shoreline, presented a majestic approach to the hotel and afforded guests a taste of controlled nature that included chairs, umbrellas, food, drink, sporting equipment, reading material, and whatever else a guest might desire. The Great Lawn was an engineered paradise, a peaceful wonderland that merely required its privileged denizens to possess loads of money.

When Jeffie spotted me walking toward him, he abandoned the women and ran into my arms. I dropped the ball and swung him around until he laughed uncontrollably. My mother yelled at me to be careful. Virginia had given up trying to inhibit our play.

As William walked up, he said, "You're not quitting already?"

"I am. I'm going to play with Jeffie. It's a beautiful day. Relax. Sit down. Enjoy the view. Lunch will be served soon."

Before leaving the hotel, I had ordered a picnic to be laid out for one in the afternoon. I checked my watch. The food and drink would arrive in less than ten minutes. I hoped that would keep William busy.

"Sit? Women sit to while away an afternoon. Men take every opportunity to challenge and improve themselves. You're lacking skills, but you can learn. You show some ability."

"How generous of you to say that," I answered evenly.

William missed the sarcasm. "It's true, you can improve. Hard work and sweat. When I was on the team, we practiced every day. It takes commitment to be good at something. Come on, we have a few more minutes until lunch arrives."

He was becoming tiresome. "To what purpose? I'm sorry, but no one plays team sports in the West. I'm going to play with my son until lunch arrives."

William laughed. "Then perhaps I can help. With a little work, I'll make him a starter for Harvard."

With that, William got on his knees in front of Jeffie and put the ball in his hands. After a lot of nonsense babbling from William that was supposed to approximate a toddler's talk, Jeffie let the ball roll out of his hands in William's direction. Everyone cheered as if this were an accomplishment. I glanced at my mother, and she gave me a don't-you-dare look. Besides disliking William, I now resented him.

Thank goodness, our picnic arrived. Three waiters spread a red-and-white checkered tablecloth over a wooden table under a tree, ironed it smooth with their hands, and then distributed cloth napkins, real silver, wine and soda bottles, baskets of food, and finally, a slender vase with fresh flowers. What could be better? A beautiful day, a grand view of the Pacific, and service that should impress even my mother. Everyone took a seat, and arms went everywhere as people poured drinks, snapped out napkins, and distributed sandwiches, chicken cooked on a spit, boiled corn on the cob, potato salad, and fruit—the perfect setting to broach a difficult topic with my mother.

I was about to ease her toward my subject when William said, "Stephen, I read your books on the train. Very fanciful. I enjoy tall tales about the Wild West but find them difficult to believe." He made a show of looking around. "From what I've seen, the West looks pretty tame."

I resisted the urge to tell William that the adventures I described were real and at least as truthful as Mark Twain's *Roughing It* or Ben Franklin's autobiography. A little embellishment helps keep the reader's interest. I thought of my books as true … and mostly accurate. William's intent was to rile me, but I wasn't going to take the bait. I glanced at Jenny, who had played a prominent, though anonymous, role in several episodes, but her expression displayed complete disinterest. Was this an act or had she not read the books? Knowing her, it was an act. Many times, I had witnessed her project personas to achieve what she wanted. If she had not become a cattle and silver baroness, she could have been an actress and easily achieved top billing.

I smiled at Virginia before saying, "Publishers insist on embellishments. I wouldn't say it was tame here, but it's safer than the tawdry neighborhoods in New York. By the way, where are you going to live? I assume Nevada."

"Nevada *and* Boston," William said with pride. "With trains, we can travel between the cities in less than a week. Railroads represent the epitome of man's ingenuity. With their unbelievable speed, we've collapsed the size of the nation. We can now traverse this entire great country in splendid comfort." He laughed. "I can't imagine traveling by horse or covered wagon. My goodness, that must have been horrid. After experiencing the comfort of your mother's car, we're going to build a private car of our own."

"Do you have interests in Boston?" I asked Jenny.

"Yes," she said with a beguiling smile. "William."

I laughed appropriately, then clarified, "I meant business interests. I know you're a sharp woman of business. You must have spotted opportunities."

"The Adams family have presented me with several prospects, but none have felt right yet. I need to consolidate my interests in Nevada before I look afield."

At the end, she dropped her façade and threw me a fleeting, nasty look. It may have been only transitory, but she made sure it lasted long enough for me to catch it. I had trespassed. She was leading William and his family along. She had no intention of letting her interests in Nevada continue to meander along without her. I could guess her game. She would occasionally go to Boston with William, but also allow William to visit his family's home without her. She might even give him enough money to invest in some Boston endeavor to give him a reason to return more often, which would please his family. I suspected that William's real role was to provide her with an excuse to fend off male advances and bestow on her the status and respectability needed to grow her Nevada-based empire.

I didn't expect William to fare well away from the civil society of Boston. Jenny's ranch house was the envy of the state, and she owned a substantial home in Carson City, but Carson City was not Boston. It occurred to me that William might expect a bustling metropolitan culture, because both cities were state capitals. Carson City, despite its name, could hardly be considered more than a small town. The Nevada capital justifiably bragged about its political prowess, robust commerce, beautiful tree-lined residential streets, and civil lifestyle, but Virginia City, only twenty miles away, epitomized the image of a rowdy and dangerous Wild West town.

"Tell me, Stephen," William said, "did you expect people to believe your story was autobiographical?"

William wouldn't let it go. Was he miffed that Jenny and I had some history? Perhaps he suspected that Jenny had been the model for the young girl who charmed everyone with a guileless act while ruthlessly destroying enemies. He could even have deciphered my oblique reference to repeated sexual assaults of the young girl and wondered if there were aspects of Jenny's past that she hid from him.

I laughed. "I certainly hope not. Novels are a serious business, but they aren't meant to be *taken* seriously. No more than stage plays. It's all an act, a great form of entertainment. I made up my stories and characters. I had great fun, and I just hope that you and others enjoy reading my books."

A glance toward Jenny confirmed that I had recovered a smidgen of her goodwill. Virginia reached over and patted my hand.

The remainder of lunch raised no more ghosts from the past, and Virginia and I excused ourselves to put Jeffie down for a nap.

As he slept, Virginia and I read in upholstered chairs that sat on either side of a large window overlooking the Pacific Ocean. She read *Little Women* by Louisa May Alcott, and I read *Twenty Thousand Leagues Under the Sea* by Jules Verne. We had different tastes.

After a peaceful, quiet period, Virginia said, "William knows."

"He suspects, but he doesn't know."

"He's an ass, not stupid."

I let my book fall into my lap. "What do you mean?"

"I mean, they've been married two months, and they just spent nearly a week together in a train car. He's been exposed to some of Jenny's sharp edges."

"So you think Jenny has already let her veil fall? I doubt it."

"Jenny achieved her objective with William. He's already in place as her husband. Now she's moved on to new goals, so she may have been careless."

"What new goals?"

"Reassembling her empire. Men have encroached, and she intends to blister their behinds."

"She's done more than that in the past."

"She has, but she's become more sophisticated. Both in manners and reprisals."

"It sounds like you two have talked. Don't become too friendly. I don't entirely trust my mother's work."

She laughed. "Agreed." Then she appeared thoughtful. "I'm not supposed to mention this, but your mother is keen to be rid of her. She wasn't specific, but Jenny has apparently been a handful."

"Perhaps ... but I'm equally certain she hasn't abandoned her intended uses for her. My mother would use the devil himself to promote the family."

"*Your* family," she pointed out.

"My family … but I've put some distance between us."

"Nearly three thousand miles."

I laughed. "Yes … and it may not be enough. As we learned this afternoon, trains have made us all neighbors."

Now she laughed. "Trains made you rich. Did you think there was no price?"

I shook my head, smiling. "Damn, my investments brought Mother closer. Should have put all my money behind Edison."

After a few more minutes of idle chatter, we returned to our books.

After a moment, she asked, "Do you want to read?"

"What else do you have in mind?"

She smiled innocently but then said something not so innocent. "Jeffie seems to sleep better in the afternoon than in the evenings. Let's see about making him a sister."

Without a conscious thought, I laid my book down and stood. I took her hand to help her out of her chair. We kissed, at first gently, and then with increasing passion. A pounding on the door interrupted our embrace. It sounded urgent. I ran to the door and flung it open to find Jenny.

Before the door opened fully, she exclaimed, "They've abducted William!"

"Abducted? Who?" I asked, bewildered.

"How the hell should I know? They only left a note."

She thrust it at me.

I read out loud. "We got your husband. $25,000 gets him back. Cash. More to come. Soon."

Jenny looked down. "Steve, they brought William's ring finger in a tobacco tin. Our wedding ring was still on it. They said they'd send more body parts if we didn't cooperate. They said—"

She broke down crying.

After clearing her throat, she continued. "They said they would send another finger in seven days, then one a day until we deliver the ransom. When he runs out of fingers, they'll send his body back to us."

"Don't worry," I said. "We'll get him back."

"But what if I don't want him back?" she wailed.

Chapter 3

I ignored her last outburst. Despite her words, she appeared genuinely distraught. Perhaps she did care for William, or perhaps the severed finger panicked her, or perhaps she was experiencing an internal conflict she found unnerving. With Jenny, one never knew. I led her by the elbow to the chair I had been sitting in. She sat with reluctance.

"How did this happen?" I asked.

"And when?" Virginia added.

"We had a tiff, and Will went for a walk ... about two hours ago ... maybe more. This note was slipped under my door not three minutes ago."

"Did you go to the law?"

"I came to you."

I looked at the note again. "This is hotel paper, available in the lobby telegraph office. Maybe someone saw who took it." I made for the door and threw over my shoulder, "Virginia, I'll order up tea service. See if you can help Jenny remember any details."

I ran down the single flight of stairs to the lobby. The telegraph office was at the front by the door. When I entered the small room, three men waited for the operator's attention. I pushed my way past them, saying I had a mortal emergency. I received a few unpleasant looks, but no one said anything. I ripped a page off the memo pad and waved it at the operator.

"In the last hour, did someone take one of these pages but not turn in a telegraph order?"

"I'll be with you in a minute," he said as he tapped away.

I almost yelled "Now!" but I had never seen an operator interrupt a transmission. I spent the next few seconds tapping the edge of the note paper against the counter. When the operator finished, he swiveled his stool toward me.

"What is the nature of your emergency?"

He must have heard my exclamation to the men in line. I thought quick. It might not be in William's interests for the news to become public. I hurriedly wrote a note on the paper I held and passed it over the counter.

He read it and started to speak, but I held up the flat of my hand. "This matter is extremely private. Would it be possible to ask these gentlemen to step out for a moment?"

After another quick glance at the note, the operator politely asked the men to step into the lobby. With minimal grumbling, they shuffled out, and I closed the door. As soon as it shut, one of the men rapped on the glass and yelled at me to hurry.

I returned to the counter and handed the operator the abductor's note. He read it and shook his head. "I didn't notice anyone today, but that doesn't mean someone didn't take a sheet. I have my back to the counter when I transmit. Also … it could have been taken earlier and kept in a pocket until needed."

"Are you aware of any other abductions at the Del Monte?"

The question made him uneasy. "You better ask the manager. I have customers to serve."

I left, convinced that his second comment was not a rationale for the first.

I found the manager taking inventory in the bar. When he finished his task, Nathanael Nelson greeted me with an amiability most people reserve for friends. Hearing my earnest request, he agreed to meet privately in his office.

Instead of a rolltop desk, Nelson used a flat desk with a surface that had been polished to a high sheen. A perfectly centered gold pen set interrupted a nearly clean desk. Three neat stacks of papers sat in a line down the right side of the desk. Shelves behind him held more documents and the type of folders used by lawyers. Photographs cluttered the wall above the shelves, and a quick glance told me they were images of famous guests. Obviously, they were meant to impress a supplicant facing Mr. Nelson as he sat behind his imposing wood barrier. In all, the expensively appointed office displayed the tidiness of a room seldom used. I took it as a sign that he might be a capable administrator, mostly out and about his hotel, ensuring that all is as it should be.

"What can I do for you, Mr. Dancy?"

"I have a matter that requires the utmost discretion, and I need your word that you won't go to the law without my approval."

"My apologies, but I can't give that assurance until I know the issue."

"It's not a crime committed by a guest, but one committed against a guest."

I saw a spasm of fear flash across his face, but he quickly regained his composure. Too quickly. What could that mean?

"Mr. Dancy, you must understand—"

I interrupted him. "You've had previous abductions, haven't you?"

"Excuse me. What are we talking about?"

"My friend has been abducted for ransom. You knew my problem before I explained it. How many abductions have there been?"

Nelson sat back and tried to appear relaxed. "Mr. Dancy, tell me what you think has happened. You say a friend has been abducted?"

I wanted to grab him by the collar and shake him, but I decided to wait until later in the meeting.

"Do I have your assurances about the law?"

"You do."

Of course. If I was right, Nelson didn't want lawmen involved any more than I did. He would want us to pay the ransom. Pay and get out of here without making a fuss. I wondered how many times this had happened before.

"My mother's ward has recently married, and they're here on a belated honeymoon. This afternoon, her husband was abducted, and a note left demanding twenty-five thousand dollars."

Now Nelson put on his concerned face. "My." He hesitated. "Do you have that much money?"

"Sir, are you in cahoots with the abductors?"

Nelson recoiled. "What? Heavens, no. Whatever gave you that idea?"

I leaned forward. "Perfect crime. You identify wealthy guests, allow the culprits ready access to your resort, and facilitate the ransom payment. The guests leave quietly, relieved to have their loved one back, and they remain silent to keep other criminals from viewing them as easy marks. Nice racket."

"No, no, you're wrong! I have nothing to do with this. Listen, I'll admit it's happened before, but I'm not involved. You must believe me. I own thirty percent of this hotel and the surrounding real estate that's been partitioned into lots. Please, I'd never jeopardize my investment by associating with an outlaw scheme. I have nothing, *nothing* to do with this."

I remained silent and maintained eye contact with Nelson until he looked down at his desk and shifted the few papers around to no purpose.

I said, "I'm not convinced. Let me ask a few questions, then I'll know if you're telling the truth." After he nodded, I asked, "How many times has this occurred before?"

"Three ... now four."

"Has the law ever been involved?"

"No."

"Did the families pay?"

"They did."

"Did the hostages go free unharmed?"

"Yes. The culprits appear to keep their word."

Nelson looked hopeful, which irked me.

I said a bit testily, "Even if we pay and remain silent, this will not end well for you. You know these abductions will keep happening. You can't keep them secret forever. Sooner or later, word will get out and the Del Monte will become a sad memory." I let him contemplate that before adding, "The swells who can afford your resort will stay away. You'll be ruined. Do you understand?"

Now he appeared distraught. "You think I didn't already know that? Let me ask you a question. Are you willing to risk your friend's life to capture these outlaws? Because putting an end to this means one of you swells needs to go to the authorities."

I thought about it. I didn't like William, but I couldn't put his life at risk without his volunteering to help capture these men. Besides, if he were injured or killed, I would have three women mad as hell at me. I'd rather face outlaws.

"No," I answered simply.

"Nor were any of the other three families. Believe me, I want to bring this to a stop, but to do that, I need to bring in the law. Every time I suggest that, I receive threats you wouldn't believe." He shook his head, looking forlorn. "I'm ruined any way you look at it."

The man suddenly had my sympathy. Jenny could easily afford the twenty-five thousand. For that matter, so could I or my mother. Do we pay and move on, leaving this poor man to eventually become the real victim of this tragedy? The smart answer was yes, but I didn't like being played as a mark. It went against my gut instincts. I had to at least explore a little more.

"Do you have any idea who's behind this?"

"What difference does it make? Are you going to shoot them all?"

"Perhaps … maybe after I get my friend back."

He laughed. "You don't look the type, and if it's who I think it is, there are lots of them, and they're mean. Meaner than anything you've encountered."

From my dress and deportment, he assumed I was an easterner, unaccustomed to the bad elements on the frontier. I wasn't going to dissuade him of that impression while I remained uncertain whether he was an accomplice.

"Tell me about them," I said.

After a short bout of nervousness, he finally shrugged and said, "There's a gang in these parts. Bad people. Very bad. Killers. Into everything. If it's illegal, they control it. No one commits any crime around here without their permission. I suspect they take a cut of every theft and robbery in the Monterey-Santa Cruz region, probably further. I don't know if they're the ones abducting rich people for ransom, but they certainly know about it and get a cut."

"Do they have a name?"

"They call themselves *la Junta Mixta*, or more commonly, just the *Junta*."

"The mixed board? What does that mean?"

"You speak Spanish?"

"*Un poco*," I responded.

"Another translation would be the joint board or joint committee. Three gangs quit fighting each other and joined up. At first, everyone thought the combination was good, because murders in the harbor area nearly came to a halt. After a while, people realized that the gangs, free of internal warfare, could prey on ordinary citizens. They got organized, and now they control everything."

"You said three gangs. Which gangs?"

"Mexican banditos, a Chinese tong that runs the wharfs, and white American outlaws." He shrugged. "Thus, the name."

There was a soft knock on the door. Nelson called out, and a girl in her teens entered.

"Mr. Dancy, this is my daughter, Rebecca."

After some perfunctory greetings, she asked, "Anything for tonight?"

Her father gave her a couple slips of paper from the shelves behind him, and she was gone.

"Tell me about these gangs," I said to put the conversation back on track.

"Monterey was the capital under the Spanish and then the Mexicans, so we have a strong Mexican presence, including *las bandas*. The shipping and fishing companies imported Chinese laborers, and the owners found it easy to use the tong to manage the crews. The white gangs were the smallest, mostly convicts who had served their time and a few outlaws who had never been caught. They may have been small in number, but their leader is shrewd. He pulled the gangs together and negotiated the truce. Rumor has it that he allowed the Mexicans to name the combined group, so he must be a good politician as well."

"Where do they operate?"

"Everywhere between Santa Cruz and Pacific Grove, but the leader wants to pull more outlaws into the Junta. He's supposedly looking at San Francisco." He shook his head. "He's ambitious."

"How much do you pay them?" I asked.

Nelson appeared taken aback. "What makes you think I pay them anything?"

"You said they were into everything criminal. That must include a protection racket."

"I'm not sure I know what that is."

"Yes, you do, but let's leave that for the time being. How can I find this leader of the white gang?"

"People don't go looking for him. Ever. He sends people to find you. If you did find him, you'd be out of your element … and outnumbered. He never meets anyone alone. He's always got mean killers around him. Ruthless men, capable of anything."

"I have friends," I said.

"A gentleman like you doesn't have the right kind of friends for men like this. My advice: Pay the ransom and go home."

"I may pay the ransom, and I certainly *will* go home." I leaned forward and lowered my voice. "If you won't tell me how to find him, at least tell me his name?"

Nelson looked down at his lap and shook his head. Eventually, he looked up at me and shrugged. "Listen, his name is unimportant." He leaned forward, hands folded, both forearms on his desk. "Stay away from him. He's a murdering cutthroat who'd skin alive his own mother if there was money to be had. These are bad people. Very bad. Pay … and get the hell out of here."

While I thought about his advice, I asked. "Who's the law in town?"

"Sheriff. No town marshal. We rely on the county because most of the population is within a square mile of where we sit."

"His name?"

"He prefers to just be called sheriff."

That seemed odd, but I'd look him up and make my own impression.

Having made my decision, I stood to leave. "All right, I'll pay."

"You've made a wise decision."

I stopped and gave him an appraising look.

After a long moment, I said, "Mr. Nelson, if you've told me the truth, you have nothing to worry about from me. But if I discover that you are mixed up in this, you'll rue the day you met me."

I left, closing the door a bit more firmly than necessary.

Chapter 4

As I opened the door to our suite, everyone leaped to their feet and spoke simultaneously.

"What did you learn?" Mother demanded.

"I hope you didn't speak to the law," Jenny said.

"Steve, is Jeffie in danger?" Virginia asked.

I held up the flat of both hands. "One at a time. Please, sit down. I'll explain everything I can."

"Why were you gone so long?" my mother asked, taking her place on a small divan. "You had us worried sick."

"I know. I'm sorry, but this is complicated. I'll tell you everything."

Which I did over the course of the next fifteen minutes. When I finished, everyone started to speak at once again, and again, I held up both hands to quiet them. After they settled down, I pointed at Jenny.

"You agreed to pay twenty-five thousand?" she asked.

"I wasn't talking to the abductors; I was talking to the hotel manager. At the moment, I want him to believe we'll pay and not make a ruckus. William's your husband, so it's your decision."

Jenny fumed. "I don't care who you were talking to, once you said we'd pay, word will get out … and you said the manager might even be an accomplice?"

"I hope word does reach the abductors. Even if you decide against paying, it's best to keep them thinking you will. It gives us time to formulate a plan."

"I don't need a plan. I'm going to Nevada to take care of my interests, William be damned."

That startled me. I knew Jenny could hide her feelings, but the couple appeared to get along fine and enjoy each other's company.

"Jenny, dear," my mother said, "I know you don't mean that. William can be—"

"I do mean it. I made a mistake marrying him. I don't care for him. He's a sniveling snob … and a blowhard to boot. Why should I pay an immense ransom to get back something I don't want?"

Mother said, "You don't really want to be rid of William. You need him."

"For what?" Jenny sneered.

"We've discussed this," my mother said patiently. "This is a man's world. An ambitious woman needs a pliant man at her side. The things you don't like about William actually make him perfect. Plus, he doesn't have the nerve to steal from you."

"Oh, I have no fear of him stealing from me—or even sticking his nose in my business—but he thinks marriage gives him the right to incessantly use my body." She was suddenly livid, as if the mention of his bedroom behavior stoked a deep repugnance. "Better if someone else kills the bastard. Let them be the one who goes to prison."

I glanced at Virginia, and she gave me a slight shake of the head. She needn't worry. I had no intention of getting in front of this raging beast. Jenny's revulsion toward sex didn't surprise me. She carried scars from several assaults that William probably knew nothing about. It did surprise me that she would admit out loud to welcoming someone else doing away with her husband. For her to shed her innocent demeanor, William must have really angered her.

My mother sighed heavily. "Jenny, I know you find your spousal obligations distasteful, but his expectations are not unreasonable. Men of his age have needs, but you certainly don't need to fulfill them. Send him out to seek fulfillment elsewhere. This is what women of position have done for centuries. Believe me, in a couple of years, there will be an unspoken agreement between you, and you'll both be pleased with the arrangement."

I admired my mother's ability to seem to have Jenny's interests at heart when she really didn't want to harm her own schemes. This was about empire. The Dancy family was a major force in New York politics and business. My wife's family possessed similar power in Philadelphia. Although neither Virginia nor I intended to support her dreams of empire, Mother expected to eventually woo us to her side. William came from a prominent Boston family, and Mother expected Jenny to extend the family connections to the distant frontier, where fresh fortunes were built daily. Poor William. He had no clue that he was a mere cog in my mother's endless connivances. No wonder I had run away from these people and chosen to live in San Diego, the furthest I could be from New York while remaining within the United States.

Jenny reluctantly turned her surly gaze on me. "You think they'll deliver him over if we pay?"

I shrugged. "They have in the past."

"Once they hand him over, then what?" she asked.

I was bewildered. "What do you mean?"

"I mean, will you chase them down and kill them?"

Virginia rose from her seat and blurted, "He'll do no such thing!"

"Jenny, quit trying to get a rise out of us," I said. "This is no time for your games. I'll not seek revenge for you, Mother, or your hapless husband. Pay or don't pay. I don't care. But don't goad me for entertainment."

Jenny dropped her chin in an apparent pout. Without moving her head, she looked up at me with an expression of contempt, but after another moment, she shook off her anger and smiled genuinely.

"You know, Steve, you may be the only one who thoroughly understands me."

No one understood Jenny thoroughly, but I understood her well enough to know she still held a grudge against me for past transgressions. I examined her and wondered if my mother understood that Jenny was very sick.

I smiled in return. "I doubt that, Jenny, but I do know that you're smart and capable … and you hate to be abused or slighted. Whatever your relationship with your husband, you'd never allow someone else to murder him."

She nodded. "I let emotions get the better of me. Of course I want William back." The sweet innocence had returned. She blithely added, "I'm willing to pay one-third of the ransom, and I presume you and your mother will gladly contribute the other two-thirds."

I almost laughed. Pure Jenny. I now suspected that this entire conversation was meant to lead to that last remark. I hesitated only a moment before saying, "Okay, as long as it's understood that I will not maraud around afterwards seeking retribution."

"I wasn't serious," she said with a grin.

"Good." I turned to Virginia. "Where's Jeffie?"

"In Juanita's bedroom."

Juanita had been Jeffie's nanny from his birth, and she accompanied us everywhere. A mature, rotund woman with a gentle spirit, she looked after Jeffie like he was her own. Because her husband had delivered Jeffie, we first thought she was a nurse, but then discovered that she helped only on occasion in his practice. Her two sons had returned to Mexico to attend Universidad Nacional Autónoma de México, the oldest university in North America. Neither had yet wed, which was why I suspected she treated Jeffie like her own grandson

I opened the door and looked in on them. Jeffie played on the floor with wooden blocks while Juanita wove a basket. I traded smiles with Juanita and stepped back into our sitting room.

"There seems to be nothing to do except wait for the next note from the abductors," I said. "I'm going to town. I need to send telegrams, and I'm not sure the hotel operator hasn't been compromised. I'm hiring guards to protect us. I'll try San Francisco for Pinkerton's."

"Thank you," Virginia said. "I'll feel safer if someone watches out for Jeffie."

"Oh, my God!" Mother exclaimed. "Don't tell me they abduct little children!"

"No, Mother, don't worry, but an ounce of caution is worth a pound of cure." I swiveled to look at Virginia. "Can I speak to you in our bedroom?"

Without a word, she stood and walked to our quarters in the three-room suite. I led her to the balcony that overlooked the ocean.

Once outside, I said, "I'm going to start wearing my .45. Can you handle a single-action .38, or do you want a Colt Lightning?"

She suddenly looked worried. "You expect trouble?"

"Trouble's already found us." I nodded toward inside. "I didn't tell them everything. William was taken by a criminal gang made up of Chinese, Mexicans, and Americans, evidently a large band of very bad men. As I said, they've pulled this extortion numerous times. I hope there's no additional danger, but until we get William back, I want hired protection … and both of us armed."

She nodded and appeared somewhat mollified. "Buy me a Lightning."

I nodded. For the last couple of years, I had worn the Colt .38 pocket pistol, but now I wanted to carry a large-caliber handgun. Virginia's personal weapon had always been the double-action Colt Lightning. She wasn't overly skilled with it, but its familiarity would give her confidence. Along with my .38 and Army Colt .45, I had also brought a '76 model Winchester.

I turned to leave.

Virginia asked, "You're not going to get involved beyond the money, are you?"

"No. For one thing, there are too many of them. For another," I put my hand on her arm, "this is not my home."

"She tricked you into paying, you know."

I laughed. "She hasn't lost any of her cleverness. God save William, if we succeed in rescuing him."

Chapter 5

If la Junta Mixta had as much power as the manager had suggested, I couldn't trust any locally hired guards. A gang with that much ambition would have already subjugated local resources, formal and informal, and probably even corrupted law enforcement. My experience had been with the Pinkerton National Detective Agency, and I had been well satisfied with their work. I had never encountered a corrupt telegraph operator, but I had a concern that the Del Monte telegrapher would tell the Junta or the hotel manager, which might be the same thing.

I found a public telegraph office a short walk away in the town proper. In short order, I sent a query to the Pinkerton's office in San Francisco, and wired my friend, Captain Joseph McAllen, recently retired from the organization. I asked McAllen if he knew people in the San Francisco office, and if he did, to recommend a team leader.

Afterwards, I went to a gun shop, where I purchased a Colt Lightning .38 for Virginia because she had left hers in San Diego. I also purchased a leather sap, a folding knife, and four boxes of ammunition. I had the store wrap them all up in brown paper cinched with twine.

Next, I walked out of a bank with four rolls of quarters. In years past, Virginia had been taught how to fight assailants with a lead-filled purse. She had kept the purse as a reminder of her close encounter with killers, but she had left it in San Diego. A few years of peaceful life, and our alertness had waned. We had become accustomed to a safe, sedate life. One of my socks loaded with quarters should serve as a reasonable substitute for her purse.

What had I left undone? Then I saw the sheriff's office. Was there something to learn there? How should I go about it? I could judge character reasonably well, but I needed a pretext to enter the office. I needed to determine if I could trust the local law, but I couldn't expose the Junta demands. I decided to stay close to reality but play a rich buffoon.

I wandered over, hefting my purchases under my left arm. As soon as I stepped into the office, two deputies moved to opposite sides of the room with their hands on their guns. Why would a gentleman walking into a sheriff's office cause anxiety? I laid my bundles on the floor.

"May I see the sheriff?"

One of the deputies stepped forward and said curtly, "State your business."

"I'm a tourist from San Diego. I was warned that this town is a hotbed of criminal enterprises. I have my family here for an extended stay, and I want assurances that we will be safe."

"You want assurances?"

They both laughed.

"Okay, you're safe. There you go. Now enjoy your stay in our town."

"Please tell the sheriff that a citizen wants to talk to him … or I will be forced to see the mayor, and I can assure you, he will see me."

"What is he, a personal friend of yours?"

They laughed again.

"No, the governor is," I lied. "Better yet, ask your boss to meet me in the bar at the Del Monte. I prefer to keep this unofficial. I'll buy the drinks, of course." I reached down for my packages, then stood up. "Deputy, also please tell him that remuneration would be considered de rigueur."

"I don't understand a damn word you just said. De what? Is that Spanish?"

"It's French and is commonly used among educated individuals." My expression became put upon. "Just tell the chief I'm willing to pay … and I pay well." I shifted my purchases to my left hand so I could open the door. "Good day, gentlemen."

I left with only their laughter assailing me. I smiled as I headed back to the hotel.

When I entered the suite, all three women were seated in the same positions as previously on the facing loveseats. But this time, only Virginia leaped to her feet. As she helped me with the packages, her eyes asked if I'd bought her preferred weapon. I nodded ever so slightly. She smiled and carried the packages into our bedroom.

My mother ordered me to keep my rifle unloaded inside the suite. I wondered what she meant until I spotted my Winchester lying across the mantel with a box of ammunition. Outside the box, a line of cartridges sat upright. Someone had relocated the vases of flowers to a side table to accommodate the rifle. The gun was well out of Jeffie's reach, so I wanted to keep it loaded. An empty rifle was nothing more than a badly designed club.

I told her it would remain unloaded for the time being, which could mean any amount of time. Virginia returned from the bedroom, but before she sat, Jenny and my mother excused themselves to return to their respective rooms.

Virginia smiled. "I want to open the packages."

After returning to the bedroom, Virginia unwrapped the brown packages as if it were Christmas morning. When she found her pistol, she immediately rummaged through the boxes for the correct caliber of ammunition. Maybe I would need to revise my impression of her barely adequate gun skills, because she thumbed open the gate and deftly loaded the Lightning. When done, she unbuttoned the back of her dress and stuffed the small pistol in the small of her back.

As she buttoned her dress, I asked, "What did you tuck that gun into?"

"While you were gone, I put a heavy leather belt under my dress."

I smiled. "Smart." Then I had to ask, "If you need it, you don't intend on unbuttoning your dress, do you?"

"Steve, if I need it, I'll rip the dress open. After all, I've had a lot of practice sewing buttons on things."

I laughed. I had previously shown impatience with her buttons.

She stood a bit straighter. "I feel better. The whole time you were gone, I kept looking at the door, wondering what I would do if one of those gangsters burst in. Your mother wouldn't let me load your rifle."

I gave her a kiss and said, "She tell you to line up those cartridges?"

"Yes. She claimed she could load the rifle before someone could bust down the door."

"She can. At least a couple of cartridges. She's handy with that heavy rifle, so if someone tries to intrude, you cover the door with your pistol while she loads."

"Why can't we load it? It's out of Jeffie's reach."

"Because I'd rather take on the bandits from la Junta Mixta than argue with my mother." I smiled to show I was kidding. "Besides, they want the money for Will before they steal another swell. We're safe for now, but I'm glad that when I leave the hotel, you'll be armed."

We kissed again. This time more seriously.

When we parted for breath, I said, "I brought you another gift."

I pulled out the rolls of quarters and handed them to her. She looked puzzled and then displeased.

"What am I supposed to do with these? For your information, Mr. Dancy, women prefer paper money. Lighter in the purse." Then her face brightened. The mention of her purse and the heft in her hand recalled her experience with the lead-filled purse in New York.

"Yes!" she exclaimed, as she ran over to the bureau and pulled out a small embroidered evening bag with a long strap.

As she attempted to rip open the first coin roll, I said, "I was going to dump them into one of my socks. Won't an evening purse look odd during the day?"

"In Philadelphia maybe, but out here, they'll assume I'm newly rich and have no idea about fashion." She smiled. "I'll flaunt it."

After she emptied all the coins into the purse, she hefted it and swung it in small circles. Then she came over and kissed me. Very seriously this time.

"You really know how to woo a girl." After a coy smile, she added, "Jeffie's in the nanny's room, and I'm not eager to rejoin Mother and Jenny."

Without a word, I walked over and locked our bedroom door.

Chapter 6

I hurriedly freshened up for my rendezvous with the county sheriff. Virginia expressed concern that one of the Junta might spot me talking to a lawman. It was a reasonable fear, but I believed I could spot anyone who didn't belong in an exclusive drinking establishment. Troublemakers stood out like a bulbous nose on a clown.

When I entered the hotel bar, I easily spotted the sheriff but saw no one else who would give me pause. He gave me a brusque nod from a table against the back wall. He was a big man, muscular, not fat. He looked like he could take care of himself. His clean-shaven face, personal grooming, and haircut belied his slovenly dress. As I sat, I could detect no body odor. I looked closer at his clothes. They were inexpensive, wrinkled, and ill-fitting, but they had been freshly washed, just not pressed. So the sheriff was clean and groomed but disheveled. What did that mean?

I vowed to be careful with this man. If he took graft, he didn't spend the money on expensive suits or commercially laundered clothing. That might mean he was smarter than the average law enforcement thug. On second thought, it could also mean that he was an unkempt slob who had recently visited a barbershop and taken a bath. I could have caught him at an opportune time, right after his weekly cleanup.

I introduced myself. "Steve Dancy."

"You can call me sheriff."

"No name?"

He stared at me.

I sat and took a casual pose. "Can I buy you a drink, Sheriff?"

"You better for keeping me waiting. Whiskey."

I signaled for the barman. I hadn't taken overly long upstairs, so if he had been truly waiting, he must have come directly over to the hotel after my visit to his office.

"I apologize," I said. "I bought a few gifts for my wife, and she wanted to open them immediately. You know women."

After ordering, he asked, "Why do you want to talk to me?"

"Well, it's difficult to explain entirely. You see—"

"Better make it short. You have the time it takes for my drink to arrive. When it does, I'll swallow it down and leave, so get to the point."

I nodded understanding. "I heard there's a gang in these parts that preys on the rich. I'm probably the richest man in this hotel, and I need protection, so I came to you." I sat straighter. "I deal only with the top man."

Only a humph in reply, and then he spent many moments appraising me.

Finally, he asked, "Who told you this?"

"A maid. One I pay handsomely for personal favors and information."

"Which maid?"

"A gentleman does not disclose such things."

Another humph and another appraisal. "Tell me what she said."

"She said the name of the gang is Spanish, but not all the members were Mexican. She said they were mean, tough men who enjoyed robbing rich Americans. They had all kinds of ways. Straight-out robbery, crooked gambling, entrapment with prostitutes, extortion, blackmail, abduction, and on and on. She warned me that my family might be at risk. That we were prime marks."

"How much did you pay this girl?"

I pretended offense. "That's none of your business."

"It is my business. She owes me half."

He said this evenly, as if it were a generally known fact. No mystery remained. The sheriff was in cahoots with la Junta Mixta.

I stammered a bit and then said, "That's between you and her."

"No," he said. "You give me my half or her name. Otherwise, we'll see how your wife likes you poking around with other women."

"I didn't come to you to be blackmailed. Your job is to protect guests in this county."

"Go to hell, tenderfoot. You don't vote in this county, nor do you pay my salary, so I owe you no obligation."

The sheriff did not believe in subtle negotiation.

I sat back in my chair and acted resigned. "How much to protect my family? And I don't mean guards. How much grease do I need to spread around so I can holiday in peace?"

"Ten thousand … plus the twenty-five thousand for your *cobarde amigo*. Oh, and another ten dollars for your tryst with the maid." He smiled wickedly. "For ten bucks, I'll let that go … this time. Never again. You tell her that."

I nodded. No subterfuge, no proclamations of civic responsibility, no thinly veiled threats. The sheriff just threw it out there. He was not afraid of getting caught. He was confident no one would challenge him. He also knew I was associated with William. I suspected that he had this county locked down tighter than a drum.

Our drinks arrived.

I took a sip and said, "You're a direct man."

"Way to get things done." He lifted his drink in a show of swallowing it down in a single gulp. "Yes or no? I have other affairs to tend to."

"Did you assemble this Junta outfit?"

He laughed. "Be thankful I'm not him. If you had approached El Jefe as rudely as you did me, he would've probably killed you on the spot." He jigged his whiskey glass again to display his impatience. "What's your answer?"

"Yes," I said, without hesitation.

He swallowed his drink and stood. "Bring the ten thousand … plus a half eagle to my office tomorrow … or more calamity will befall your family."

"Tomorrow? That's a lot of cash on such short notice. I need time to transfer funds to a local bank," I pleaded. "Wait, please. Sit for another moment."

He reluctantly sat, making a hurry-up gesture.

"If I pay thirty-five thousand, my friend will be returned with no additional harm, and all six of us will remain fully protected for the entire length of our stay?"

"That ransom is between you and the abductors. Not my business. We were negotiating your continued protection only."

I acted nervous. "But ... but you knew the amount of the ransom."

"Nothing happens hereabouts without me knowing about it. However, that is none of my doing."

I noisily sipped my drink before stuttering, "But like the maid, you take a cut?"

He laughed uproariously. "Damn, tenderfoot, this ain't no court of law." He laughed some more. "Tell you what. I'll give you two days to get my retainer. Pay in two days, or your pretty wife will enjoy a present from me."

He stood and left the bar, laughing all the way.

Chapter 7

I found the hotel manager in the kitchen, inspecting the preparations for supper. As soon as Nelson saw me, he broke free of his task and motioned me to follow. He led me to his office.

After the door closed, he said, "What do you want? I can't be seen talking to you all the time."

"I just met the sheriff. He demanded another ten thousand to guarantee the safety of my entire party for the length of our stay."

He sighed. "You went to the sheriff? That was stupid."

"Perhaps." For some reason, the accusation made me uncomfortable. "I told him I'd pay, but I need to understand his relationship with la Junta Mixta before I deliver a pile of cash to him. Can he deliver what he promised, or is he a fringe player?"

Nelson seemed perplexed by the question.

He stood to escort me out of his office. "I can't talk to you."

I wore the .38 pocket pistol under my suit coat. I flipped my jacket open so he could see that I was armed. He hesitated, and for a moment I thought he would throw me out of his office and his hotel.

I pushed. "Mr. Nelson, you *will* talk to me. Have you ever heard of Sean Washburn of Nevada? Or George Carson?"

"Of course. They were notorious gunmen, both killed plying their trade."

"I killed them."

His head snapped back in surprise at either the idea of my being a killer or my bluntness.

He sat down and stared appraisingly at me. "I don't believe you. Even if it's true, it won't mean a damn thing if you square off against the sheriff."

"You're scared of him," I accused.

"As you should be."

Now it was my turn to stare. I came to a decision. "I'm unconvinced you're trustworthy, but I have no choice. I need allies. I'm asking, will you work with me? It's the only way to save your hotel and real estate investments."

"I'm sorry, no," Nelson answered.

I leaned across the desk. "It's an error to fear the sheriff more than me."

"You're one man; he has dozens. More." He pointed at my coat. "There are more of them than there are bullets in that gun."

I stayed quiet for a dramatic moment. "Good point. To save bullets, I won't shoot you in the thigh." I stood. "Instead, I'll tell the sheriff that I know about the series of abductions … and I learned it from you. I'll tell him you confided everything to me. That ought to put him in a foul mood."

As I turned to go, he leaped to his feet. "No! You'd be signing my death warrant. Wait! Please!"

I turned back but did not sit. "All I want is information. I won't involve you. If I win, you get to operate your business safely. If they kill me, your cooperation goes to the grave with me. You win whichever way it goes."

He thought about what I'd said, and I'm sure he wondered if I'd really tell the sheriff about a made-up betrayal. I suspected my hard act may have fallen short. I probably didn't look like a man evil enough to cause him real harm. At this point, I just tried to appear impassive.

"Have you no conscience?" Nelson finally asked. "No mercy?"

"Not when it comes to protecting my family," I said in as flat a tone as I could muster.

He plopped against the chair back. "Very well. What do you want to know?"

"Let's start with my first question: Can the sheriff deliver what he promised, or is he a fringe player?"

"Damn, you're naïve. You'll never beat them." Heavy sigh. "My only hope is that he kills you before you squeal."

"I'll fight to the end. I won't allow myself to be captured."

I meant what I said, but it sounded like bravado.

Nelson sighed again in resignation. "The sheriff runs the whole damn thing. He's the one who brought the different bands of outlaws together. After he brokered a truce among the criminal elements, he cajoled the legitimate businessmen and townsfolk. Told them he had crime in the county under control. I think he even ordered the Junta to lay low for a while. When he ran for sheriff, he won in a landslide. Everyone knew he had previously led a small group of outlaws, but they hoped a bad man could corral other bad men. Instead, he uses his office and deputies to protect the Junta. The next sheriff north is part of the Junta as well. Monterey and Santa Cruz counties belong to him." He gave me a look that said I was a fool. "The sheriff's the big boss man. And you went right into his web."

"He told me El Jefe runs the gang."

"That's what they call the Mexican leader. The sheriff keeps the peace within the Junta by allowing El Jefe to playact as boss. He controls the gang by being unpredictable and, on occasion, by being savage as hell. The sheriff promotes himself to the Mexicans and Chinese as the great protector. He tells them that they can get away with murder, but only as long as he remains sheriff, the white man who guarantees that the law won't interfere with their looting. Make no mistake, every member of la Junta Mixta bows to his wishes. They're scared to death of him. He's erratic … and a stone-cold killer."

"When we met, I asked you for the name of the leader. If you'd told me, I wouldn't look such a fool."

"How was I supposed to know you'd poke around where you shouldn't? The man is dangerous. I was trying to protect you."

"How do you know so much about the way he runs his business?"

Nelson hesitated but evidently decided he might as well tell me everything. "I have the trust of the Chinese tong."

That took me by surprise. "The tong? How?"

"I used Chinese laborers to build this hotel. The tong was very helpful … and I return favors."

I nodded understanding. "Back to my question; will the sheriff keep his word?"

Nelson appeared nervous. "You shouldn't have gone to him … and you shouldn't have said you'd pay a separate extortion."

"Why?"

"Because he's trying to figure out just how much he can take from you. He threw out the ten thousand number to see how you'd react. Once you yielded to his demand, he'll want more … all you got … maybe even your lives."

I hesitated only a second and then stood. "I'm leaving."

"My office?"

"No, this town. I won't keep my family in the vicinity of that jackal."

"Wait. You can't leave. What about your friend? He'll kill him so slow, he'll beg to die."

"I met that so-called friend for the first time last night. He's a boorish snob. I have a wife and son to think about. William's wife has enough money to handle the ransom. I don't need to remain here."

"He's already set the hook. You're a big catch. He won't let you go. He'll have men at the train station, and I doubt you can get out by horse."

"I arrived by carriage," I muttered.

"There's only one road out of here. Whether you go north or south on El Camino Real, you'll be spotted by highwaymen beholden to the Junta. If the sheriff has put out the word, you'll be under the gun as soon as they spot you."

"I can handle *los fracasos*."

"Losers? Misfits? No. You're wrong. These are capable brutes. They'll haul you right back to his lair. You won't stand a chance … and neither will your family. A bloody gunfight will put your family in dire jeopardy."

I sat back down. Damn it. A couple of years ago, I would never have dodged a threat from a petty tyrant, but I had grown comfortable … and soft. I liked it. I liked having a family, I liked our home overlooking the ocean, and I liked going to sleep unafraid. I had put my hellion days behind me. And more than anything else, I enjoyed the absence of gunplay in my life.

There had to be a peaceful way out of this mess.

I asked, "Beyond the abductions, how often have they extorted money from rich guests?"

He fidgeted before saying, "First time last month. I think they discovered a new racket by accident. They took this eastern buffoon for nearly a hundred thousand. Got it all, his entire wealth. It started when that numbskull got drunk one night and bragged about stealing his mother's jewelry. She lives in Chicago, and after he stole her diamonds and gold, he ran out here because it was out of the way, but he could still live the easy life at the hotel. A perfect mark. He couldn't report the extortion to the law outside of Santa Cruz, and if he took it to the local sheriff, one of his deputies would write up a complaint and send the fool packing."

"But I could report an extortion scheme to law outside of Monterey. I've already bragged about having connections in Sacramento, and my money comes fair and square. Wouldn't the sheriff be concerned?"

Nelson appeared to think. Finally, he said, "You have a point. The sheriff doesn't want to alert outside parties, so … you might be okay."

I heard the hesitation.

"What're you not telling me?" I demanded.

He played for a moment with a pen on his desk. When he spoke, he sounded sympathetic. "The sheriff will think this through. Stealing from an admitted thief is pretty safe, almost as safe as stealing from a dead man."

I had already thought of that. "You told me he was clever, that he would think this through. If rich men keep disappearing in Monterey, he'll kill the golden goose."

"That's why he'll try to discover how rich you are first. If you're rich enough, he can play you and leave the other swells alone. Quit the game for an extended period. Maybe he'll fix a sailing accident or something else that can be explained away. Robbed by highwaymen on the way out of town. Maybe you just disappear between here and Paso Robles. If the prize is large enough, the sheriff will figure out a way to grab it."

"What happened to the hundred thousand he stole from that sucker last month? That's enough money to live well for a lifetime."

"Decent, not well. The sheriff has rich tastes. His house in San Francisco would impress your mother. He struts around that town wearing the finest clothes, rides in a custom carriage, attends opening nights, and eats in the best restaurants. Don't let that disheveled local attire fool you. He's a meticulous man with refined tastes. And besides, there are over two hundred members of the la Junta Mixta. The sheriff keeps the lion's share, but he spreads cash around to all the gang members. He may have walked away with tens of thousands, but that's not enough for his appetites."

"How do you know about San Francisco?" I asked. "Surely the tong didn't tell you that."

"I go there frequently for business. Most of my supplies, labor, and furnishings come from San Francisco. I saw him at a charity event looking different, sounding different, and using a different name. I got out of there before he spotted me, but my curiosity had been piqued. I hired someone to look into him. He lives a double life. In San Francisco, he's known as a gentleman, one of the Knob Hill idle rich." He glanced toward the closed door. "If he has the chance, my bet is he'll go for the big take … especially if it's enough to skedaddle for good. If the prize is large enough to live the high life, he won't share with his friends. He doesn't care about Monterey or la Junta Mixta. Francis only cares about Francis."

"Francis?"

"Let me guess, he told you to call him sheriff?"

I nodded. "If he doesn't like Francis, why don't people call him Frank?"

"Because Francis is his last name, first name Henry. Before he won the election, everyone called him Hank, at least to his face."

I thought a minute before asking, "San Francisco's not that far away. What will El Jefe and the tong do when he skips town with all the loot?"

"That's a problem for sure, one that the sheriff will need to resolve before committing this piece of larceny."

I thought about all of this and became dejected. "So all the outlaws in the region have been consolidated into a single gang, and the law's in bed with them. In fact, it leads them. Combined forces of over two hundred. The main culprit is a greedy, duly elected sheriff who fancies himself a dandy, and to top it off, he kills indiscriminately."

Nelson looked sympathetic. "That's about it. He likes the high life, controls every outlaw within a hundred miles, and is on the lookout for a big stake." He hesitated. "One more thing. He's exceptionally handy with a gun. Also knives and fists. If fighting's involved, he's mastered the tools and techniques. Worse, he applies his skill with a rage you would never believe until you see it."

"He sounds crazy."

"Now you're beginning to understand."

I stood to leave.

"What are you going to do?" he asked.

I shrugged. "Not sure. What do you think I should do?"

"If you can figure out a way to run," he said from behind his desk, "run like hell."

Chapter 8

I didn't trust Nelson enough to totally confide in him. He sounded forthright, but he was probably hiding some level of complicity, so I didn't mention wiring for help.

I left the hotel grounds and headed to the public telegraph office to see if I had any replies to my telegrams. As I walked, I wondered what I should do with the Pinkerton team when it arrived? Fight? Use it to guard our escape? I didn't know. I loved my family, San Diego, and my life of late. I had extravagant investment plans that provided me with all the excitement I needed, and I didn't want to do anything that would put my family in additional danger. Prior to my marriage, the combination of wanderlust, male companionship, and exciting adventures made life thrilling, but when I looked back, I realized I'd had an unhealthy disregard for my well-being. In truth, I was lucky to have survived in one piece.

With no line at Western Union, I was immediately handed a telegram. Unfolding it, I discovered that the San Francisco Pinkerton's office couldn't commit a team of six agents until the end of the following week. There was additional hedging that made me feel uneasy. Damn it.

Joseph McAllen had not responded to my telegram. That did not come unexpected. McAllen's ranch was twelve miles outside of Durango, and he wouldn't see my telegram until he made a trip into town.

McAllen and I had traded letters for the past few years. He had settled into his retirement from Pinkerton's, and his horse ranch had prospered better than expected. Both the U.S. Army and Pinkerton's were steady customers. His major problem wasn't sales but breeding enough horses to satisfy these organizations' insatiable desire for good stock.

I had an inspiration and sent a telegram to McAllen's former wife. Perhaps she would find someone to ride out to his ranch to deliver my plea for help.

I wrote Pinkerton's a second telegram instructing them to send the crew as soon as possible, and if one or more agents were available in advance of the full team, they should be dispatched immediately. I considered sending another wire to McAllen, asking him to use his influence with the San Francisco office, but he would do whatever he could after reading my first telegram. A bit dejected, I had nothing more to do except return to the hotel.

Two beefy deputies waited for me on the boardwalk.

One said, "Come with us. The sheriff wants to see ya."

"Give the sheriff my apologies, but I'm busy."

I started to step around them.

They quickly blocked my path. "This ain't no request."

"Are you arresting me?" I asked.

The talkative one smiled. "If need be. Like nothin' better."

I didn't want a fight, so after a moment, I said, "Lead the way."

"No sirree. Ya know the way. Go in front."

Both men let their hands hang lazily alongside their pistols and appeared competent with a sidearm. I might be able to get them to back down if I pulled my gun on them, but an altercation might ruin any chance of getting my family safely out of town. I sauntered the two blocks over to the sheriff's office.

When we entered, the sheriff stood by the window, watching the street. Another deputy leaned against a wall by a rack of rifles.

"Did he give you any trouble?" the sheriff asked.

My escort chuckled. "He wanted to but thought better of it."

He waved them away and said, "Leave. I want to teach him a private lesson."

All three stepped out onto the boardwalk and closed the door.

The sheriff turned on me. "Do not try my patience. Understand?"

"Are you a patient man?" I asked.

"Like that. Don't sass me."

"What do you want, Sheriff? I'm busy."

"Busy hiring Pinkertons? Asking friends for help? Help doing what? I made you a fair offer, and instead you seek protection by armed ruffians. Well, that offer's gone. Now, it'll cost you more. Lots more."

Nelson had been right. The sheriff's first number had just been a probe to find out if I would pay more than the ransom. More worrisome, he had corrupted the Western Union operators, or more probably the office manager. Now he would use my call for help to raise the stakes.

"If you get William Adams delivered back to his wife without any further harm, we'll talk about a reward for doing your duty."

"You shit, I define my duties, not you," the sheriff said angrily. "And they do not include charging into the barrio with guns blazing to save some rich dandelion. That's outside my jurisdiction. My advice is to pay the ransom. I'm talking about what's in my jurisdiction, and that's the rest of your party. The whole damn Dancy clan. You, your highfalutin mother, your wife, your child, and that other pretty young thing. Since you went against my wishes, ten thousand will no longer cut it."

I grew pissed and demanded, "Why should I pay a sheriff to enforce the law?"

The next thing I knew, my shoulder and then head were slammed against the wall. I never saw the sheriff's fist heading toward my temple. He hit hard. And fast.

He shoved me up against the wall with his forearm and screamed into my face. "You shit! You'll pay me and pay me plenty, or I'll beat you to death! Then I'll give your wife to my deputies to do with as they like and sell your son to the tong! The young girl's mine. No more squeals for help to the pretend police. They can't help you. They won't help you. The agent in charge does what I tell him. Believe it! He knows better than to go against me." He grabbed me by the lapels. "Do you understand, greenhorn?"

"I understand." I responded in a tone that conveyed that I understood something other than what he intended.

He gave me a final shove and let go.

Free of his grip, my first instinct was to draw my gun, but I merely straightened my suit jacket.

"What do you want?" I asked.

"How much is your life worth?" he asked. "How about that old queen's life? Your wife's? Your darling little boy? Even that pretty wench with you? How much will you pay for all of you to see next Christmas?"

"Hell, I don't know, I can't even get together the ten thousand you already asked for."

He stepped toward me and yelled in my face. "Bullshit! I checked. Your damn mother's one of the grand dames of New York City. She's the matriarch of the Dancy clan, a family notoriously powerful in the East and richer than Charles Crocker. You don't do bad yourself. Heard you have a big house on Coronado Island and lots of other investments. Don't lie to me, you son of a bitch, you can get the money … and you will."

I needed time.

I said, "Not right away. You think we have idle cash sitting around? It's invested in enterprises. It takes time to liquidate investments or borrow funds and even more time for a local bank to amass the cash so we can give it to you."

The sheriff's tone suddenly became conversational. "Not here. Not local. The deposit will be made to a San Francisco bank."

"I don't have that kind of money in San Francisco either."

"Well, get money there … or else."

We had come to the hard part. I asked, "How much?"

"How much are your lives worth?" he asked again.

He wanted me to open the bidding.

"Fifty … beyond the twenty-five for William," I offered.

"Good number … for each."

"What? Each? You can't be serious."

"Oh, I'm serious … deadly serious. Two hundred and fifty thousand for the five of you. I want the money in my account at the Bank of California in San Francisco. I'll give you my account information when the money is ready for transfer. You'll be free to go only after the money has been deposited. Have I made myself clear?"

"You want to extort me for a quarter million dollars? That's unbelievable."

"Believe it. But since I'm not heartless, and it's a large sum, I'll give you a week."

"You've got to be joking," I said. "I can't come up with that amount of money, especially not in such a short time."

"Ask mommy. I'm sure she'll help. If not—" He shrugged.

"Give me at least two weeks."

He pretended to think, then ghoulishly grinned before speaking conversationally again. "No, and if you ask again, I'll gouge out one of your eyes. In fact, if you do anything I disapprove of, anything, I'll gouge out one of your eyes, and if you do something again, I'll gouge out one of your son's eyes." Now his sneer turned even more grotesque. "Let's see, I can keep that up for five eyes … and then I start cutting off hands." He paused dramatically. "But it will never get that far, will it?"

I answered simply, "No."

"Good, we understand each other. Now one more thing—"

He jabbed me hard straight in my nose. Blood gushed.

"I told my deputies I needed to give you a private lesson." He laughed. "Now they'll see evidence of my work. By the way, they're not to know anything about our arrangement. Nothing. If you say one word to anyone not named Dancy … pop goes one of your eyes. Got it?"

I said yes through a handkerchief I held to my bloody nose.

"Good. Now go. You need that attended to, and you need to talk to mommy."

He laughed uproariously. "By the way, be grateful you didn't try to pull that peashooter on me. If you had, I would have shot you several times in the leg, and you wouldn't be walking back to your hotel. And by the way, tell anyone who asks that you walked into a door."

He laughed some more as he opened the office door for me.

"Mighty careless of you," he said, "mighty careless."

Chapter 9

I fumed. My bleeding nose wasn't a big deal, but my head throbbed with an awful ache where the sheriff had hit me. Nelson had been right about his fighting skills, or at least correct about his expertise at fisticuffs. The man punched like an experienced boxer. I possessed a natural ability with guns, but I had never shown a similar bent with other fighting forms. In the future, I would be more heavily armed and keep the sheriff at a distance.

I fumed not because of my disgrace, but because of his threats to my family. Nelson was right about something else. After getting his money, the sheriff would kill me. He didn't want his newfound wealth questioned, nor did he want to worry about my seeking revenge. It hadn't sounded like he had learned about my skill with guns, but he knew I tried to hire professionals. He would worry that if I ever got to a safe haven, I would hire gunmen to go after him. Killing me would stop that threat. To be really safe, he would dispose of my entire family so my wife couldn't raise a ruckus about my death.

I knew from previous experience that I couldn't fight an entire band of outlaws. Bad men came in an endless supply. I needed to kill the sheriff. Cut off the head. That would take a single bullet. After he fell, the rest of the la Junta Mixta would splinter into competing gangs that would be easier to handle, especially if I could put real law enforcement in place. Knowing the solution and putting it in place, however, were two different things.

I hustled through the lobby, shaking off hotel staff who saw my blood and offered help. When I burst into our suite, Virginia leaped to her feet, but I rushed past her and into the bathroom. I needed to wash off my humiliation. She followed on my footsteps into the sparkling, modern room. Indoor plumbing was one of the Hotel Del Monte's advertised luxuries, although some used to outhouses still couldn't countenance relieving themselves in the home.

I examined my face in the mirror. The bleeding had stopped, and I tweaked my nose to confirm that it wasn't broken. Just a bloody nose. Then I rubbed my temple. It hurt far more. The sheriff had taken a full swing at the side of my face but had only jabbed my nose. I'd live. As I washed up, I decided to abandon the well-off gentry look. I went into the bedroom to change clothes. After I redressed in trail clothing, I slung my .45 around my waist. I walked back to the sitting room and loaded my Winchester. Even in the suite, I felt a need to be fully armed. I didn't want to be taken by surprise again. Ever.

Judging by the look on her face, my being heavily armed worried Virginia. After a hurried explanation, I got up and poured a small whiskey. Drinking from now on would be moderate. I sat down and looked at the closed door to the second bedroom.

Virginia saw my glance. "Juanita took Jeffie outside to play." The worried look was still there. "Do you think it's safe?"

"Probably … for now … but I still don't want to chance it." I stood. "Let's go get them and bring them back inside."

I started for the door, but she put a restraining hand on my forearm. "No need. I told her to stay under our window."

Our room was on the second floor. Virginia went to the window, which was already open, and called down to the nanny to bring Jeffie back to the room because I had returned. There was no panic in her voice. Smart woman.

She sat back down. "What will we do?"

"Gather up money while we search out other options." I thought a moment. "Perhaps one of us ought to be with Jeffie at all times."

"Since Will was abducted, I've let Juanita take him outdoors only for short spells and then stay by the window so I could hear their chatter. I suppose I need to go with them now."

"Armed," I said.

"Of course." She appeared contemplative. "I want a shooting lesson."

"Not a good idea. If they see us shooting, it will forewarn them we intend to fight."

"Do we intend to fight?" she asked.

"What do you think?"

She hesitated. "We'd better. If they take us for that much money, they won't want us around to cause mischief afterwards."

I nodded. "My thinking as well. I need to kill the sheriff."

"Do you think that will be enough?"

"No … la Junta Mixta is large and could become more dangerous without stern leadership." Before continuing, I thought about what I had said. "The sheriff knew about my telegrams, so clearly he has this whole town under his thumb. By my measure of the man, he wouldn't share this type of information with his rival gang members. The Junta without the sheriff would be physically threatening but wouldn't be privy to our every move. Which reminds me, don't trust anyone on the hotel staff."

She nodded understanding.

I shook my head. "We need soldiers and allies in place before I move on the sheriff."

"No help from the Pinkertons?"

"Doubt it. I don't think he was bluffing about his ability to stop a team from being dispatched. According to the hotel manager, he spends a good amount of time in San Francisco."

"Damn," she said. "Then how do we get help?"

"First task: find a way to communicate with Joseph. If I can wire him unbeknownst to the sheriff, he can get us a Pinkerton team from Denver."

"How? The telegraph operator is on the sheriff's payroll."

"At Western Union. Probably here at the hotel as well." I got up and paced. "Mail is too slow, so it has to be the telegraph." I thought some more. "I have the best chance of sending messages privately inside the hotel. I don't trust the manager, so I need to control him."

"You have an idea?"

"An inkling. If I—"

Jeffie and his nanny burst into the room, and he did his stiff-leg little run until he reached my arms. I swung him around, and he laughed and laughed. I felt the start of tears in my eyes. How dare anyone threaten my child? I couldn't bear to see harm come to him. While I breathed, no one would sell him into tong slavery. I looked at Virginia and could see the same commitment in her eyes.

I put Jeffie down, and we hugged and babbled at each other for another minute; then I waved Virginia over to the corner of the room.

"Are you armed?" I asked.

She nodded.

"I'm going down to see the manager. Lock the door. I shouldn't be long, and I won't leave the hotel."

She nodded again, and I left. I waited in the hall until I heard the door lock.

I was frightened. I couldn't communicate with the outside world, and my only ally was a hotel manager I didn't trust. That wasn't quite true. I had been in deadly fights with Virginia at my side. I couldn't think of anyone I'd trust more to protect our child. They would have to go through her to get to Jeffie. And that's what scared me. They would go through her. She would put up a good fight, but in the end, these were nasty men, and they came in bunches. If I allowed her to be caught alone, she would die horribly.

I needed to get back to our room as quickly as possible.

I ran down the flight of stairs.

Chapter 10

This time, I found the manager in the restaurant, chatting with guests. I took a table, and when he surveyed the dining room, I surreptitiously waved him over. He appeared put upon but came over nonetheless. I indicated that he should sit.

"What happened to your face?" he asked.

"I had a run-in with the sheriff. He knew I had sent a telegram to hire a team of Pinkertons."

His expression didn't change. He said nothing.

"Western Union strictly enforces privacy, so the fact that the sheriff corrupted a telegraphist surprised me."

Nelson finally spoke. "A man needs to shelter and feed his family. Livelihood depends on not crossing the sheriff."

"You're saying the sheriff can threaten a man's job, even if he works for one of the largest corporations in the world."

"At the very least. He can do more." He glanced around the room. "What do you want?"

I hadn't mentioned which telegraph office, so I assumed that Nelson suspected that his own operator might have been compromised.

I ignored his question. "How do you communicate with your partners and investors?"

"That's none of your business," Nelson answered.

"I want to make it my business. If you knew or suspected that the sheriff read your correspondence, you'd find another way to communicate.

You're too good of a manager to do otherwise. I want to use your personal operator."

"I have no idea what you're talking about."

"You do." I leaned in a bit closer. "Did you learn to tap out messages yourself or hire someone else and hide him on your staff?"

"Again, none of your business."

"Remember, we're in this together. I take on the sheriff and the Junta, and you give me information. That's our deal."

He sat there stone-faced.

What was I missing? If I ran the hotel, I would secretly hire a telegraphist and squirrel him away in another part of the hotel operations. He hadn't denied that he had done the same. I would also send my personal messages after the hotel telegraph office closed. No one would be the wiser. Since a Pinkerton team would help us get out of this mess, why the reluctance to share his operator?

Then it hit me. "Rebecca!"

"What are you talking about?" Nelson exclaimed, too sharply.

"Your daughter is your personal telegraphist. You gave her messages to key the first time we met. That's why you're so protective of your clandestine communication. You don't want her further involved."

He stood. "I have to see to my other guests. Have a good day, Mr. Dancy."

"Sit, please. Let's discuss this. We both want free of the Junta." I waited as he considered his options. After a moment, I added, "Please, sit. It's in Rebecca's interest."

He sat. "What if you guessed correctly? What do you expect?"

"A few messages to people who can help. Nothing on a regular basis. In fact, after she sends these, I suggest you keep your own correspondence to a minimum. If I figured this out, so will the sheriff."

He looked worried. "I can't have that."

I thought a second. "I'll send some wires by your regular operator as well. I need to start actions to raise money, and I'll embed a few calls for help. The sheriff expects me to try something, and that might keep him from sniffing around too much."

He remained worried but nodded. "All right. Give me the telegrams."

I wrote them on the spot, handed them over, and then left to compose new ones for official transmission.

It took me a half hour to send telegrams to New York and San Diego, instructing my banks to accumulate cash in my accounts by selling assets. I wrote that transfer instructions would follow in a few days. I sent these messages from the Western Union office in town. I sent additional wires from the hotel so the sheriff would assume I thought the hotel operator remained uncompromised.

When I stepped out of the hotel telegraph office, I spotted two deputies in the lobby. They gave me a hard look and waved me over.

Not again.

Chapter 11

I headed toward the stairs, ignoring the deputies. They quickstepped over to block my path, their hands resting on gun butts. The leader nodded his head sideways to indicate that we go outside. I examined the lobby, and our little drama had not escaped the notice of other guests. As casually as possible, I wandered out into the gardens. The deputies motioned toward a high hedge, away from the strollers' pathway.

This was the second time they had waylaid me exiting a telegraph office. How had they known so quickly? I knew the answer. If they watched the single road leaving town, they certainly kept an eye on the two telegraph offices.

After we were somewhat concealed behind a hedge, I asked, "What do you want?"

"Who'd ya send telegrams to?"

"Go ask the sheriff. I'm getting something for him."

"Rod, go check."

The deputy named Rod disappeared.

The one who remained with me appeared pleased with himself.

I said, "What's your name?"

"Call me sir." He looked even more pleased with himself. "Got yerself a grown man's gun, I see. Know how to use it, greenhorn?"

"Since your friend's gone, you better hope not."

"Go ahead. Try yer hand."

I took a step closer to him. "You're not too bright if you're trying to goad me into a fight. If you—"

"Don't you dare threaten me, greenhorn … and back off."

I leaned in closer to him. "Listen for a second, win or lose … you lose in the end. If I win, you die right now. If you win, the sheriff will kill you for messing up his plans." I got an inspiration. "Do you know his plans? Has he shared them with you? Do you have an inkling of how much money he's demanding from me? If not, you might want to think about why he's keeping it secret. I can assure you, it's lots. Enough that killing me would make him madder than you've ever seen him. Now think about it, do you want to cause all that anger?"

"Go to hell."

He had muttered the affront and appeared unsure of himself. I felt relief. If I acted smart, my family would be safe until I transferred the money. This meant I had some degree of control over the sheriff and his underlings … for a time. I had to figure out how to use this leverage to stall until I could turn the tables on them.

The other deputy returned with a couple of my messages in his hand.

Rod said, "This halfwit tried to summon Pinks again." He looked at me. "That's a mistake, asshole."

"I hope you left my other messages with the operator. If you didn't, your boss will be unhappy."

"Oh, I left them. But I got bad news for you. The sheriff said if you tried any shenanigans, we're to beat on you." He waved the pieces of paper. "Well, Sam, we're gonna have a bit of fun."

"Did you read the other messages?" I asked.

"Yes, cupcake. Some gibberish to banks." A thought seemed to occur to him. "What have you got cooking with the sheriff?"

"Something you ought to know about." I remained casual and confident. "Interesting that you don't."

"Yer stallin'," Sam said.

He looked around to make sure we were alone.

In a flash, I drew my Colt and jammed it into Rod's chest just below the ribcage, and then in one smooth motion, swung the gun around until the barrel hit Sam above his hairline. Both men went down.

"Explain that to the sheriff."

I walked away.

Chapter 12

"Will they tell the sheriff?" Virginia asked.

"Having personally witnessed his raw anger, I doubt it. They'll tell him they roughed me up but left no visible marks."

Virginia glanced toward the closed bedroom door, looking contemplative. Jeffie was playing in the bedroom under the nanny's watchful eye. I knew she wondered if roughing up Sam and Rod had put our family in greater danger.

I said evenly, "Listen, the next week was going to be hell unless I pushed back. These two are assigned to keep me in line. I need elbow room, so I shoved back, showed them I knew how to handle a gun. Now they know I'm armed and fast, and they'll back off a bit … I hope. I admit it was a risk, but I believe it was one worth taking."

"Steve, they thought you were innocent gentry, now they know different. I'm not sure that was smart. Perhaps your pride made you act rashly."

Her comment irritated me. "Virginia, I wasn't keen on another beating. Besides, if I'm right, and they keep quiet, only those two deputies will know."

"*If* you're right." She stepped closer to me to give her words more force. "If not, the sheriff will disarm you, even if he needs to use all of his deputies. You won't be able to protect yourself … or us. Then where will we be?"

"Dependent on armed women, I suppose." I smiled to show I was kidding. "Listen, it may have been a mistake, but it's done now. Let me fetch mother and Jenny so they can catch up."

She smiled wanly and waved me on my way. I left the suite grateful to escape.

Was she right? Had I bludgeoned Sam and Rod due to mere pride … or fear of a beating? I wasn't sure. I knew I hadn't thought about my actions in advance. I had acted on instinct. That thought made me feel better. Since arriving in the West, I had acted on instinct and had few regrets. I trusted my instincts. Thinking too much in the face of grave danger was a mistake.

I wasn't afraid of Sam and Rod, not even together. They were capable deputies, but they weren't experienced with people confident enough to push back. Their demeanor or badges cowed the people they bullied, but I had handled harder outlaws, plus I knew I could hire the best lawyers in California if need be. Being honest with myself, I had to admit that I moved through life with self-assurance due to my wealth. I could buy myself out of legal jeopardy if one of my encounters with these deputies went too far. The sheriff was a different story. My instincts told me that the sheriff would prefer to vanquish me outside of legal norms. He would never allow his office to restrict his course of action.

I expected to find Jenny and my mother together, but they were in their separate rooms. I gathered up both women and nudged them toward our room. Jenny was in a foul mood, while my mother brooded. As we approached our door, Jenny demanded a pistol, and my mother wanted my rifle. I guess I had been prescient about depending on armed women.

When we had all gathered in my suite, Virginia ordered tea service from the floor steward, which arrived by the time I had explained recent events.

After I finished, my mother said, "You should have hit the sheriff, not a couple of witless underlings."

"I disagree," I said. "When I draw on the sheriff, it can only be to kill him."

"Humph," she responded. "Then I guess we are not in disagreement." She poured herself some tea. "So what's our next move?"

I looked from Jenny to Virginia to my mother.

"I sowed doubt into the minds of the two deputies," I said. "They must be wondering what the sheriff is up to. I suggest we use the same strategy on a much larger scale. The Junta is fragile, a cobbled-together association of three gangs with nothing in common but territory. We need to shake them up. Get them to distrust each other … and the sheriff. After all, he's stealing a quarter million dollars from us without sharing. It should be—"

"Excuse me," my mother said. "You don't intend to pay him, do you?"

"Only as a last resort."

"No, Son, you will not pay that man. Not one cent. Not for William, not for us. Never. Nothing. The Dancys are not marks. You may pretend until we find an angle to beat them, but between us, in this room, we must understand that come what may, we will never pay. If we pay, there will be no end, or if there is, that end will deprive us of more than money."

I looked at Jenny. She hesitated only a second. "I agree with your mother. Even if we pay, it won't end well. That includes ransoming William. I want him back, but I won't be made a fool."

"Well, then," I said, "Mother's right. We have no disagreement. We can't pay, but I didn't want to appear insensitive to William's plight. If the larceny had not escalated, I would've recommended paying the ransom, but not now. This is too much money for the sheriff to leave us alone after we pay. We're rich. We can hire thugs to take our revenge. And if word gets back to other gang members, they'll hunt him down and kill him for the double cross."

Virginia said, "I hate to be the wet blanket, but what if the sheriff discloses his scheme to the rest of the gang? Shares the bounty?"

"He won't," I said.

I sounded more certain than I felt. If the sheriff revealed his plans to the Junta, I had no way to drive a wedge between the gang members. I needed him to betray his partners.

"How will you start?" Mother asked.

"With the tong. The hotel manager has access to them, and they're probably the most distrustful of the sheriff." I shifted in my seat. "Mother, would you ask the manager to set up a meeting? He's nervous because I visit him so often."

She leaped to her feet. "At last, something to do. Of course I'll see him. Anything to get out of this room."

She headed for the door, but I stopped her and gave her precise instructions about what I wanted.

When I'd finished, she said, "Son, do you think this is my first negotiation? By the way, I'm going with you to meet the tong."

"No. This will be dangerous."

"If it weren't, it wouldn't be worth doing." She gave me an exasperated look. "Virginia has to stay to protect my grandchild, and Jenny needs to wait for the ransom instructions. I'm a matronly old woman. I'll put these gangsters at ease. I'll also take the little pistol of yours. I'd prefer something with more heft, but that pocket pistol will be easier to conceal."

"You're going to run this engagement, aren't you?"

She patted my forearm. "Don't worry, sweetie, I'll continue to let you pretend to be the man of the house."

We both smiled, and she waltzed out the door.

Chapter 13

The Monterey wharf area assaulted the senses. Scruffy people scurried about, boats squeaked against the docks, hand trucks were moved to and fro, and exasperated orders were yelled at the top of lungs. A general commotion gave the district an aura of excitement and energy mixed with tawdriness. To top it off, everything stank of rotting sea life, and the gutters ran with blood-red water. To my surprise, my prim and proper mother actually seemed to enjoy it.

In the morning, Mother had used Nate Nelson as an intermediary to negotiate a meeting with the tong while I met with a local banker to prepare for the transfer of ransom funds. After the midday meal, we had set out for our rendezvous. Nelson had assigned us a boy in his early teens to guide us, and he led us out the rear of the hotel through an employee entrance to a waiting cabriolet. I assumed that the deputies continued to stand guard in the lobby, but I kept a watchful eye in case someone spotted us sneaking out. I believed that we had made it to the wharf area without being seen.

The boy took us to a narrow alleyway, pointed to our destination, and then left. We would be on our own. I had serious concerns about our safety, but my mother seemed to be treating the whole episode like a grand adventure. We had dressed casually. I wore Levi denims, a cotton shirt, a waistcoat, boots, and a derby. My mother wore the least fancy clothing she had, a gingham skirt with a printed blouse. She called this her western outfit, but she had bought it in New York and had it tailored, so it failed to look anything like frontier garb. She also carried my .38 hidden in the folds of her skirt. I had thrown on my light coat so I could stuff my .45 into my belt behind my back. I wanted to be armed but didn't want to make the tong nervous.

Our teenage guide had pointed out a tin shed at the end of a filthy, garbage-strewn alley. We knocked on the tin door and heard a human grunt that we took as permission to enter. When the door creaked open, we saw a shabby, unadorned room. Three slight men sat on backless stools. I saw no weapons, but I had been told that even unarmed Chinese tong members could be dangerous in close quarters. We were waved toward a couple of additional stools facing the men.

When the door closed on its own, the shanty became nearly dark.

Sitting, I asked, "Do you speak English?"

"I speak English," the man on the left said.

The only light came from two small dirt-encrusted windows, so I had a hard time discerning their expressions. The men on the left and right were young, probably in their twenties, but the man in the middle appeared older, intelligent, and wary. None appeared threatening, but the hotel manager had warned me that the tong possessed unusual fighting skills and could inflict damage on a victim with little warning. I also tried to appear nonthreatening. As I adjusted to the low light, I could begin to make out facial expressions … but I kept my eyes on the central figure, who I assumed to be in charge.

I said, "Thank you for seeing us. My name is Steve Dancy, and this is my mother."

I waited a beat for them to introduce themselves, but they remained stone-faced and stone-postured. I decided I might as well get the meeting rolling.

"I've had discussions with the sheriff." Still no response. "Are you aware of them?"

The young man who had originally spoken said, "Many people talk to sheriff." He shrugged. "We may know or not. What did you discuss?"

"Money. Mine … and how much he wanted me to give him."

"Why did you come to see us? If you have disagreement, go back to sheriff."

"I understand you're partners with the sheriff, and I don't believe he intends to share this blackmail money with you."

"We know all about it," he said flatly.

I leaned forward, elbows on knees. "The abduction ... sure. That's small. This is much bigger. He has not even shared this scheme with his deputies."

After a very quiet moment, the three men conducted a whispered conference in Chinese

When they finished, our translator asked, "What you expect of us?"

Before I could formulate an answer, my mother said, "We expect you to get angry that he's dealing behind your back," she smiled sweetly, "and then kill him for us."

The tong leader laughed, and then, after a moment of confusion, the two younger men joined in the laughter.

The older man spoke in English. "Ma'am. I admire directness. However—" Now it was his turn to smile. "Why should we kill partner? Now we know about transaction, we will simply demand our share."

My mother asked, "You're not upset that he intended a double cross?"

The tong leader shrugged. "He is outlaw. He steals. That is what outlaws do." He laughed at his own humor. "But thank you for information."

This meeting was not going as I had hoped. These unnamed Chinese didn't trust the sheriff, but they trusted us even less. They would use our information to elbow their way to a share of the deal, but they weren't going to challenge the status quo. I had to give them a reason to join with us against a member of their own gang. Unfortunately, I had no idea what would get them to switch sides. I didn't know how to convince them to help me, but the men facing me knew what was important to them. I had to get them to tell me.

"It's about more than money," I said. "He intends to run away with the money." I let that sink in, then added, "You would no longer have the protection of the law."

The tong leader appeared unconcerned. "Where he run? To fancy house in San Francisco? We know everything happen in that city. My brothers in Hip Sing tell me. If he run there, they get money back ... just before he sink in bay."

"He knows that," I said simply.

The tong leader's eyes betrayed him. They flickered open just a bit as the realization of what I had said hit him. He became contemplative.

"You think sheriff plan kill me." He remained quiet for another moment. "Blame Mexicans. Start old war. Headless tong easy prey for Mexican banditos." Again, a quiet, stoic moment. "This no good for tong. I talk to El Jefe."

Damn. I wanted to turn the three legs of the gang against each other. The sheriff wanted to instigate a fight between the tong and El Jefe's people. The leader of the tong wanted to defend himself by banding with the Mexicans against the American outlaws. We all wanted to turn two legs of the Junta against the third. I was at a loss.

Then Mother spoke up. "Do you have brethren in New York?"

"Hip Sing?"

"Yes," she answered.

"You know Hip Sing?" the leader asked.

I turned and looked at my mother. I was curious to know the answer as well.

My mother seemed comfortable when she answered. "No one builds in New York without working with one of the tongs. I deal with Mack Lee."

"We met," he said, "many years ago. When I first came to America. I came to Monterey to start a tong. He went east."

"He has troubles now," my mother said matter-of-factly. "I believe he's in jail."

"How you know?"

"I left New York a week ago. He was arrested for a brutal murder. They threw the body off a rooftop into a crowded street. It upset people. I doubt he's been released."

The leader nodded. "I know about arrest … and jail. Not free … but trial soon. Without witnesses, he will win at trial."

"I doubt it. The body splatted at the feet of an alderman's wife, and the alderman got the newspapers riled. Now everyone wants Mack Lee to rot forever in prison."

"I know this too." His expression changed slightly. "Why you bring this up?"

"I can free him," she said.

"You?" He cocked an eyebrow at her. "How?"

"Friends in Tammany Hall. It will be difficult, but it can be done."

"You have price?"

"Work with us to destroy the sheriff."

Another whispered conference.

The man in the middle said, "What you want us to do?"

My mother turned toward me to answer.

I said, "Three things. First, when we act against the sheriff, don't retaliate against us."

He nodded.

"Two, if El Jefe comes after us, you give us protection. Negotiate first … but fight if necessary."

After a third whispered conference, the tong leader said, "You pay double ransom for friend. We use money to … *negotiate* with El Jefe. Money first. Cash."

This time I nodded and received a nod in return.

"Three, bottle up the sheriff's men who are not deputies. The American outlaws without a badge."

"What mean "bottle up"?"

"It means find out where they are and keep them there. Don't let them join the fight."

"Hardest for last," he muttered. "Sheriff's men not in one place. Scattered. Let me think."

Another whispered conference in their strange language.

At one point, it seemed that a question came up, and the leader turned to me. "Can we kill?"

I didn't hesitate. "Yes."

More discussion.

Finally, the leader turned to me and said, "After Mack Lee free, we kill three or four of outlaws in sleep. The rest may run." He shrugged his narrow shoulders. "May not. Best can do."

I nodded.

"You take care of sheriff and deputies. Agree?"

I held out my hand, and we shook.

Chapter 14

"Can you free this Mack Lee?" I asked my mother.

She gave me a dismissive glance. "I wouldn't have said I could if I couldn't. I thought briefly about doing it before leaving New York."

We were in a rented cabriolet on our way back to the hotel. The driver stood behind the semi-enclosed passenger compartment, and the clopping of horse hooves against paving stones and other noises meant he couldn't hear our conversation.

"Before you left? Why would you use political capital for a tong leader?"

"I didn't. I said I'd thought about it because I know how to work with him. I need Chinese laborers, and he gets me the best and keeps them working. Without him, I'm left with unruly dregs, or I need to start building a relationship with his successor … or another tong. That's not easy … with Chinese, it takes time."

"You'd let a criminal loose? And I'm sure he has other interests besides laborers."

"Oh, he does. Some highly distasteful, as a matter of fact. He traffics in all forms of human foibles … and human beings." She shifted in her seat and looked me in the eye. "If you had another enticement, you should have spoken up."

"No, you're right. I didn't have anything." I tried to gauge my feelings before speaking again. "Mother, I appreciate your help, but I'm startled by how far you're willing to go."

"No, you're not. You assume I'll stoop to the vilest undertakings to advance the family. But I have limits. I didn't spring Mack Lee before I left because some aspects of his business are as bad as they come. Now I need to get him released to save us. He's unscrupulous and violent. I'm not eager to bring him back into my business dealings."

"I didn't know you were experienced in dealing with Chinese," I said. "Why didn't you have an underling do that?"

"I tried, but then Lee would send an underling who could never commit until he received Lee's approval. Negotiations went back and forth, back and forth. Weeks and months went by. If I wanted decisive action, I had to deal with Lee directly."

I nodded understanding. "How do you think this meeting went?"

"As good as you could expect. You have the Dancy knack for negotiating. You want my advice?"

"I do."

"First, the Chinese are honest in their business dealings. They keep their word … unless it will cause them to be disloyal to their tong. The tong comes before all else. All else. Don't think you can get them to turn on each other like American outlaws might. They won't. If our contract doesn't require them to go against their tong, they'll be trustworthy. They'll always—"

"Wait a minute, you said contract."

"Good, you were listening. These men work in the shadows. Their businesses deal with the worst depravities. They don't write things down, so their word is their bond. And if you want to see your child's next birthday, your word better be your bond as well."

"But they can break their word if a conflict develops between our contract and the tong's well-being?"

"Exactly … and before you ask, no, you are not allowed the same luxury. You cannot choose your clan over your contract."

"That doesn't sound like their word is their bond," I said.

"Stephen, it's rare for a good-faith contract to interfere with allegiance to the tong. Just don't try to get them to turn on each other. It won't work. Understood?"

"Yes." I thought. "I mean, no. Does that include la Junta Mixta?"

"If it did, they would have told us in the meeting. If you listen carefully, you'll find they are forthright in their dealings."

"I thought the Chinese were inscrutable."

She sighed. "In motives. They seldom tell you why they take a certain action or want something. They don't share their inner thinking with people outside the tong. You have to guess. They want you guessing. I've found it best to just get on with my end of the agreement and ignore their motivations and long-term plans. You'll probably guess wrong anyway."

"Can they handle El Jefe and his people?" I asked. "I didn't see any guns."

"Never underestimate them. They look small and weak, but they're gangsters of the worst sort. Deadly gangsters, I might add. They're not going to fight him; they're going to bribe him. With our money. They'll probably offer him five thousand to sit out this fight. They'll go higher, but not to the full twenty-five. They're pretty sure they can buy him for less."

"How do you know?"

"It's how they work. Besides, if they needed more, they would have asked for more. The Chinese have been merchants and traders for thousands of years. They're shrewd ... and the toughest negotiators in the world. When they broker a deal, they always take a cut." She looked out of the buggy to see how close we were to the hotel. When she returned her attention to me, she added, "They know El Jefe's price."

"You said we have to keep our side of the deal. Did we offer anything other than the twenty-five thousand dollars and getting Mack Lee out of jail?"

"Stephen, I'm proud of you. That's a good question. The answer is yes ... yes, you did. First, we still owe the twenty-five thousand for William, but most important, you promised to take care of the sheriff and his deputies. That's part of the contract. They assume from what you said that you would kill him. You may get away with not killing all the deputies, but the sheriff is the threat you promised to eliminate."

"What if I get him arrested?"

"Men in jail can still give orders to their gang. They want him dead."

"I didn't hear that."

"Son, tongs *always* kill their enemies. Sometimes their families as well. The lynchpin to this deal is your promise to take care of the sheriff. The Chinese can be subtle to a fault. You need to listen carefully."

"I guess you got pretty good at it."

"I did. It took years and a few expensive mistakes, but I learned how to read them. I had to … or leave the New York construction business. My first mistakes seared caution into my soul."

I heard a change in the sound of the horse's hooves. We were on a gravel drive. I looked out the window to confirm that we were at the rear of the hotel so we could sneak in unnoticed. The boy from the hotel had instructed me to use the servants' entrance.

As the driver pulled up, Mother said, "Cheer up, Son. We did well. William will be fine if we live up to our end of the bargain. We eliminated the threat from the Mexican and Chinese sides of the Junta for one tenth of what the sheriff demanded." She grimaced slightly. "Getting Mack Lee out will be distasteful, not difficult."

She started to climb out, then swiveled back to face me with a smile.

"Son, get the tong's money together. In the meantime, I'll walk over and shoot the sheriff."

I must have looked startled, because she smiled before adding, "Then we can enjoy the remainder of our vacation in peace."

Chapter 15

I didn't find my mother's quip funny. This situation was on me, and I needed to deal with the sheriff. *Deal* was such a soft word. I needed to kill him. Unbeknownst to me, I had entered into a contract to do this ugly deed. Did I still have the fortitude for a life or death gunfight? I didn't know. A few years of peaceful family life had made me soft. The truth was, I had grown to like calmness. I no longer wanted to use guns to take on the West's bad men. There were too damn many of them. But … the sheriff and his men had threatened my family. I had no choice. I needed to toughen up again. I needed to get ready to fight. Mentally and physically.

I let my mother walk ahead as I stopped a bellman pulling luggage from a storeroom.

"Son," I said, "is there anywhere around here to practice shooting?"

"Just ride into the country," he said. "Or go to Cypress Point and shoot toward the ocean. Nobody's around. I used to do that all the time with school friends."

"Thank you." I handed him a silver dollar. "Could you arrange for a buggy at the back door in one hour?"

The dollar disappeared into his pants pocket as if he were an illusionist. "Of course, sir."

I turned and almost bumped into my mother, who had come back to see what had delayed me. She put a restraining hand on the bellman's arm before he could scurry away.

"Make that a carriage large enough for four," she said. "And make it three hours."

"Why large enough for four?" I asked.

"Jenny and I will come along."

I nodded. "Okay, then why three hours? I'll be hungry for supper."

"We'll make a picnic supper out of our little excursion to the shoreline. In the meantime, we need to visit a gun shop and get provisioned. I want my own Winchester, and Jenny wants a derringer and a pocket pistol."

"When did all this get decided?"

"Just now. Come on."

She waved me forward, and we marched up the staff staircase to the second floor.

Virginia and Jenny were waiting for us in our sitting room. Jeffie waddled around on the floor, Juanita hovering close behind to remove breakable items from his grabby little hands.

As we sat, Jenny handed my mother a note. She read it wordlessly and handed it to me. It was the ransom instructions. By the end of the week, they wanted the money delivered to a ship at the wharf named *La Virgen de Guadalupe*. We were not to board, just to throw a carpetbag filled with money onto the deck. The note warned that if we wanted to see William alive again, we should turn our backs on the boat and walk away. If any of us were spotted prior to the drop off, they would have their throat slit, and William would lose a hand. If anyone set foot on the boat, William would lose a foot. After the money was counted, William would be set free to return to the hotel.

"What do you think?" my mother asked.

"I think someone is trying to blame El Jefe for this abduction," I answered.

"Why do you say that?" she asked.

Juanita, rounding the couch in pursuit of Jeffie, answered before I could. "*La Virgen de Guadalupe* is the patron saint of Mexico."

I nodded agreement. "I don't think it's a coincidence that they used a ship with that name. My guess is that either the tong or the sheriff did this abduction and selected this particular ship to shift blame."

"What does it matter?" Jenny asked flatly.

"Probably doesn't," I said. "Unless we get an opportunity for retribution or arrest."

Jenny swung her head in my direction. "If there's to be retribution, the whole lot of them will be in my sights."

My mother said, "You can't kill them all, my dear."

"Why not?" Jenny asked.

Her tone said she was not kidding.

To change to a more reasonable subject, Mother and I explained our meeting with the tong. As we talked, we tried to ignore Jeffie as best we could, but I finally lifted him into my arms. After a hug, I tried to continue, but Jeffie made it difficult by covering my face with wet, sloppy kisses. I gave my mother a furtive look, and she finished the description of our meeting.

By this time, Jeffie had settled down to sit quietly on my lap with an arm around my neck. Juanita started to come over, but I gave her a slight shake of my head, and she returned to her chair. I liked Jeffie in my lap. It reminded me of what was really important. I didn't need to destroy the Junta, only to protect my family and get everyone home safe.

My mother caught my attention when I heard mention of a gun shop. Since I had already bought Virginia the weapon of her choice, it was decided that she would remain behind to protect Jeffie and the nanny.

A thought occurred to me.

"Juanita," I said, "are you okay with what's going on here?"

"Si, Señor, I understand," she answered. "Jeffie is my charge. I will protect him."

"Thank you, Juanita, but that wasn't what I meant. None of this is your doing. We've put you in danger. You should be safe on the hotel grounds, but there is more risk than you bargained for when you hired on with us."

She reached into her dress and pulled out a paring knife with the edge wrapped in a piece of burlap.

"Don't worry, Señor Dancy, I will not let anything bad happen to your son or wife."

I was torn. I admired and needed her courage, but I felt guilty for putting her in this position.

My mother resolved the issue by saying, "Son, give Juanita a raise. She deserves it. Now let's get over to that gun shop. The sooner we go, the sooner we'll return."

I walked over and put a ten-dollar gold coin in Juanita's hand.

"Thank you," I said.

She appeared surprised by the weight of the coin, but before she could say anything, my mother interjected, "I said a raise, not a reward. Good help is hard to find, and I've watched this young lady for two days. She deserves a permanent raise."

I laughed. "In case you haven't noticed, Juanita, my mother's the boss. Keep that. You'll also get a two dollar a week raise for as long as you stay in our employ."

Juanita smiled and then curtsied to my mother.

Great. My money, but Mother gets the credit.

Chapter 16

The trip to the gun shop went faster than I had expected. I selected a few gunsmith tools, a few extra parts, and loads of ammunition. Usually, women take forever to shop, but these women knew exactly what weapons they preferred. My mother selected a '73 model Winchester, and Jenny bought a Smith & Wesson .32 and a Remington .44 derringer. I wondered what it said about their personalities that my mother wanted a long-range weapon, but Jenny wanted two handguns that required close-in work.

By using the hotel staff door, we returned without being noticed. The women wanted to change clothes, so I told them I would go to the bar for a drink. I wanted my watchers to spot me occasionally, or they might guess that I was sneaking out. I found the same two deputies sitting at opposite ends of the lobby. I waved them over, and we met in the middle of the large room.

"I hope there are no grudges," I said.

Sam answered. "We gotta job to do, but once it's done, no tellin' what kind of trouble ya might run into."

"Let me apologize. I was angry, but not at you two. You were just a handy target. If you'll allow me to make amends, I'd like to buy you a drink."

The two deputies looked dubiously at each other, so I added, "Listen, I came down for a drink. You have no idea what's it's like to be cooped up with a bunch of women. You can watch from another table or join me. I don't care. The drink offer's good either way."

Sam, the talkative deputy, shrugged, "Yep, we'll have a drink. Beer only. Ya ain't gettin' us drunk."

After we sat at a corner table, I ordered two beers and a whiskey. When our drinks arrived, I noticed Sam gave my whiskey a jealous glance.

I took a healthy sip before saying, "About an hour ago, we received the ransom instructions."

"Not our business," Sam said.

"What is your business?" I asked.

"Makin' sure ya behave."

"Fair enough. Well, just so you know, the hotel is packing us a picnic supper, and we're going down to the seashore to enjoy the sunset. I'll buy you beer but not supper, so bring your own food. The women will be with me, so I'd appreciate it if you kept an eye on me from a distance. I don't want to make them nervous. Are you okay with that?"

"When?" Sam asked.

"As soon as the woman do whatever they do before they leave a hotel."

Sam laughed. "Plenty of time to finish this beer … and maybe another."

To maintain the light moment, I laughed at his feeble quip.

Rod said, "Hey, tenderfoot, we're not getting to be friends here."

"But we don't need to be at loggerheads either." I looked at Sam. "Listen, I'm sorry I poked you with my gun." I turned to Rod. "And I'm sorry I hit you with my pistol Rod. That's not like me. I'm a businessman, not a fighter. I want you men to know I'll never do that again."

"Seemed pretty handy with that hog leg," Sam said warily.

"I practice a lot. Just for fun. I've never shot at a person. Have you men used your guns in life or death situations?" When they glanced at each other, I added, "What's that like?"

"Different than shootin' at cans, that's fer sure," Sam said. "Nerves play with yer aim. Gotta be steady when yer target is shootin' back."

I looked down at my drink and shook my head. "I admire that. You men are brave … and you earn every dollar the county pays you."

I saw another brief eye contact between the men. Their income from the county was nothing compared to their share that came from the Junta enterprises. Without being obvious, I wanted to discover if the doubt I had put in their minds about the sheriff had fermented or flitted away.

"We're not your friend, and we aren't fools," Rod said. "What the hell're you after?"

Evidently, Rod was the smart one. "I want to get my family home safe. I'll pay whatever I need to. I'm willing to slip some your way if you let me leave Monterey peaceably."

"We do what the sheriff says," Rod answered.

I decided to take a chance. "Even if he's dealing behind your back?"

"Ya said somethin' like that before," Sam said. "Thunk on it. The sheriff'll tell us in his own time. He don't always tell us everythin' early on."

"Listen, you may have misunderstood me. I'm not asking you to go against the sheriff. I just don't want you to do anything on your own that will hurt me or my family. If you can forget our little scuffle and promise me that, I'll give you each an extra grand."

"Extra from what?" Rod asked warily.

Damn. Rod was too damn smart for my good.

"Extra over your deputy pay," I said. "But I want something more. I want some elbow room."

Rod stared me down. "Elbow room to do what?"

"Send a telegram or two, talk to—"

"No," Rod said firmly. "That would be against our orders. We'll forget that scuffle, as you call it, and … if you satisfy the sheriff … we'll let you go, but that's all you get for a lousy grand. If the sheriff's working on a big payday, we'll get our share like always. You can't sow doubts in our minds, and you can't bribe us with a lousy thousand dollars." He swallowed the last of his beer. "And not for free beer neither."

Rod and Sam got up and moved to another table. I waved my glass at the barkeep for another whiskey.

I had underestimated these men. Sam's unschooled speech caused me to assume that both men were uneducated, but Rod's quietness hid intelligence and leadership. He was the one in charge. I sipped my whiskey and vowed not to be careless again. These men needed to be handled like sweaty dynamite.

Chapter 17

I had alerted the two deputies to our planned excursion, so I ordered the carriage brought around front. The sheriff's men had to see us periodically, or they would barge into our suites to confirm that we hadn't left the hotel. I especially didn't want them barging in on Juanita and Jeffie. The best way of protecting my son was to lure the deputies along with us. I also wanted them to feel comfortable that they had a close eye on us, because I was sure there would be occasions when I would need to sneak away without their notice.

"What about them seeing us shoot?" Jenny asked.

"If we don't make a big thing out of it, they won't see it as unusual. People shoot at picnics all the time. I already told them I practice a lot. If they ask, I'll say you were afraid and wanted to learn to shoot to protect yourself from outlaws."

"I already know how to shoot," my mother said.

Her boast was not unfounded. She had won a shooting contest in Carson City a few years before, and I had discovered that she had frequently gone shooting with my father before he died. Virginia believed herself good with a gun, and with years of practice, she had become adequate. I doubted Jenny was skillful, but it didn't matter, because she liked to get eyeball to eyeball with her victim.

"I agree, you shoot well," I said. "So if our watchers are nearby, I'd like you to shoot only enough to sight in your rifle."

She nodded, and I could tell she understood that the deputies would be unimpressed with Jenny's or Virginia's shooting.

Mother carried a satchel filled with handguns, and Virginia carried another bag with the ammunition and my few gunsmith tools. I carried two rifles wrapped in a blanket. No need getting the guests excited by us traipsing through the lobby with an arsenal.

The two-horse carriage was well-crafted and luxurious, befitting a class resort. The Del Monte had already loaded our picnic supper, and a quick inspection confirmed that we would have a lavish cold meal with excellent chilled white wine. As we traveled a dirt road for a little over two miles to Cypress Point, I spotted the deputies on horseback only occasionally. They rode well to the rear and would, I hoped, watch us from a good distance.

Cypress Point was a beautiful, narrow piece of craggy shoreline extending out more than a hundred yards over the sea. Cypress trees grew directly out of rocky cliffs fifty feet above the breaking waves. The expansive view, rhythmic sound of surf, and warm, still air promised an exceptional picnic. We had to park the carriage away from the peninsula that jutted into the Pacific Ocean and carry our picnic and guns across a narrow land bridge to a grassy spot above the crashing waves. If our situation hadn't been dire, the evening would have been grand.

I examined the area beyond where we had stopped the carriage. Our driver, as instructed, stayed with it. I spotted the deputies behind a rock outcropping over a hundred yards away. Good. If they stayed there, they would be too far away to see how well any of us shot. Plus, if we sat on blankets as we ate, the slope would keep us below their line of sight. That was as much privacy as we could expect outside of our rooms.

After we had spread out, Mother examined her new rifle.

"Son, I wish you could modify this Winchester. I like the way your rifle handles."

As requested, I had bought her a model '73, but she had won the Nevada shooting contest using my heavier '76 model. My father had owned a gun store and taught me gunsmithing. I reached out and took the rifle from her. After checking it thoroughly, I handed it back.

"It appears to be a good, basic model. I'll work on it some when we get back to the hotel, but it ought to serve you fine the way it is."

"Let's see how it shoots. I'll go first."

She deftly loaded the rifle and stood facing the ocean. With little fanfare, she fired three times in quick succession. A thick tree limb at the ocean's edge vibrated with each shot. She sat back down.

"You're right. It's serviceable the way it is. You can leave it be."

I smiled. "You haven't lost any of your skill. Nice shooting."

"May I shoot the two gentlemen behind the rock up there?" she asked, a lilt in her voice to indicate she was kidding.

I laughed. "Perhaps, but not this evening."

"My turn," Virginia said, leaping to her feet.

I handed her the Colt Lightning and a box of .38s. After loading, she shot at the same big heavy branch, which was nearly fifty yards away. She missed with all her shots. Not surprising, because she was using a pistol instead of a rifle.

"Virginia, pick a closer target," I said. "A pistol's not a good weapon for that range."

"I already know how to shoot up close. If the outlaws are that far away, I want to hit them."

"Wait for them to get closer," I offered lightheartedly.

She angrily whirled on me. "Wait for them to get closer? Closer to Jeffie? No, Mr. Dancy. I want to keep them at bay."

"You'll be forewarning them that you're armed. Better to keep them unawares until they're within range."

She shot her finger out and pointed at the tree. "Can you hit that tree?"

I looked at it. Drew my gun slowly and held it with two hands, aligning the branch with my front sight. I squeezed off a round. Missed.

"You missed on purpose. You're the best shot McAllen ever saw, and he's seen a lot. You can hit that branch, and I want you to teach me how to hit it."

I was tempted to say that we hadn't brought enough ammunition, but she was already too angry to provoke her further.

I sighed and took aim again. It took me three shots, but I finally hit the branch.

"I was honestly trying," I said. "You need a rifle for a shot like that."

"I can hit it," Jenny said.

"With what?" I asked sarcastically.

She held aloft the derringer. "Half eagle?"

"You're on," I said.

Before I'd finished the statement, Jenny marched off toward the tree. When she got inside ten feet, she extended her arm and put a .44 right into the branch.

We all laughed. Virginia's anger vanished, and my mother hooted. Damn, what had I gotten myself into? Four armed women, counting Juanita with her tiny paring knife, against the largest outlaw gang in California.

I looked at Virginia, and she smiled at me before walking to within twenty feet of the branch. While Virginia shot, I checked on the deputies. They stood behind the rock outcropping, seemingly uninterested in what we were doing. They made no move to come closer. If they had noticed my mother's shooting, they would have wanted to remain behind cover.

After nearly an hour of shooting, we ate supper. The Del Monte had packed cold ham, fried chicken, assorted breads, various cheeses, noodle salad, potato salad, beans with bacon, chocolate cake, apple pie, and four bottles of French wine. We lounged on blankets, eating and drinking and watching a magnificent sunset. Neither my mother nor Jenny had seen the sun set into the ocean, so it was a special evening. We all laughed and temporarily forgot our predicament. Perhaps wine enhanced the experience, but I felt relaxed for the first time in days.

"Did you save enough for me?"

The sheriff's voice caused chills to run up my spine.

Chapter 18

I moved slow. I did not want to alarm the sheriff. Smart move. When I turned enough to see behind me, I was looking straight into the barrel of a gun.

"As a matter of fact, we do have enough food for you. Fix yourself a plate."

Virginia nervously rummaged around the picnic basket but sat back on her haunches and shook her head. No additional clean plates. The sheriff reached over to jerk Jenny's plate right out of her hand.

"You don't mind if I use this, do you, darling?"

It was not a question.

"Go ahead," Jenny said evenly, "but if you break it, you owe the hotel two bits."

He held the plate in his left hand, leaving his right free to hold his cocked pistol.

"Why don't you take your hand off that derringer, sweetheart," the sheriff said to Jenny. "I'd hate to spread your pretty little brains all over this scenic picnic."

Jenny, smiling seductively, slowly raised her hand away from the folds in her skirt.

"I bet you can shoot left-handed, darling," the sheriff said. "Move your other hand so I can see it's empty."

Now Jenny's expression turned furious, but she withdrew her other hand. The sheriff grinned. That was unsettling. I preferred my opponents to bluster, not smile confidently at me. After Jenny folded both hands in her lap, he handed the plate to my mother and told her to fill it.

My mother took the plate and said, "We're all armed." She plopped some potato salad onto the plate. "I see only one of you."

"That's because it's gotten darker. My deputies have you covered … and you're lit nicely against that setting sun. Just sit very still, and you can all return to the hotel together."

We sat very still. The sheriff reached around to extract Jenny's two pistols from her heavily pleated skirt and tossed them into one of our picnic baskets. I admired the sheriff's instincts. He sensed that Jenny was the most coldblooded of the group. Next, he took my mother's Winchester and leaned it against a tree out of reach. After disarming Virginia, he stood over me and stared. I peered inland and could discern a rifle barrel pointed at me from a nearby swale. I had been mistaken. He didn't think Jenny was the most dangerous. He wanted me to go for my sidearm.

He smiled, or rather smirked. "Did you buy enough ammunition? It didn't sound like you used four boxes, but hell, I got here after the festivities had already started."

"My gun's loaded, if that's what you're asking," I said.

"Naw, figured that." He laughed. "Just showing off. Wanted you to know that I know exactly what you bought at the gun shop." His smirk turned sinister. "I know everything that happens in my town. Everything."

I assumed that the Junta ran a protection racket in the area and that businesses were required to report customer doings, especially the doings at a gun shop. The sheriff would want to know which civilians may have been pushed too far.

"May I stand?" I asked. "My neck hurts looking up at you."

"Slowly, with your arms out wide."

I gradually got to my feet and reached down to take the filled plate from my mother. I faced the sheriff. I used my right hand to hold the plate but didn't offer it to the sheriff. Holding something in your gun hand appeared unthreatening, but it really did not slow down a draw. Especially after some practice. I casually shuffled a bit to my right, trying to peer around the sheriff.

The sheriff looked at the plate.

When he looked up, he said, "You still have your gun. I hear you're pretty quick."

There went my hope that Sam and Rod hadn't disclosed our little encounter.

I shrugged. "I know how to shoot, but I've never been in a fight."

He nodded toward the tree we had used as a target. "Trees don't shoot back. Much different when your target sends lead your way." He now smiled genuinely. "My advice, don't be a hero. Most heroes die. Instead, be a gentleman and remove your gun slowly with two fingers and hand it to me."

"Do you want your supper?" I asked, shifting slightly more to my right.

"You shove that plate at me, and you're dead." Then he had another thought. "And if you drop that plate, you're dead."

I maintained eye contact with the sheriff, remaining still.

"I'm going to reach over and take your gun. Don't budge, or I'll kill you."

I tried to keep my voice flat. "No."

He stopped reaching forward, apparently startled. "What do you mean, no?"

I kept my voice low and steady. "I mean you may not have my gun."

"You numbskull. No matter how fast you are, my man has a rifle pointed at your heart. The trigger is probably halfway pulled. All I need to do is flick my finger, and you're dead."

I held the plate steady in front of me. "Not unless he shoots through you." He looked behind himself. I had shifted my position until his body shielded me from his bushwhacker.

Now it was my turn. "If you move, I'll kill you."

He turned back toward me with an appraising look. Finally, he said, "Possibly, but my man will kill your wife and mother."

"What do you say, Mother?"

"Kill him now, Son, while you have the advantage."

"What advantage? You're holding a damn plate in your gun hand, and even if you weren't, I could kill you before you even thought about going for your gun. And by the way, I've been in lots of fights. Won them all. That's what we in the West call a real advantage."

"Show me," I said.

He flinched. He recovered quick, but I spotted it. This was new behavior from me, and it appeared he didn't know how to react. What did I want to happen? I wasn't sure. I had reacted on instinct. I pushed the thought from my head and focused attention on the sheriff. In a gunfight, thinking was bad. Talking worse. Every sense, nerve, and brain cell had to concentrate on the task at hand. Winning.

I saw capitulation in the sheriff's eyes. "Nice show, Mr. Dancy. You know I won't kill you before I get my money. You have until the end of the week." He grinned wide. "Then we'll see."

He turned and marched into the fading light.

My mother said, "You should have killed him when you had him in front of you."

I should have. I would have if my mother had been within reach of her rifle. Unarmed, the women were sitting ducks silhouetted against a glowing sky. Would the deputy have shot? Given time to think, he may have wondered how much he owed a demised paymaster, but in the moment, he might have automatically reacted to orders. Most probably, he would have killed me and anyone else who crawled toward a gun. I couldn't risk the life of my son's mother.

I dropped the plate and drew my gun. I had it out and cocked before the plate hit the ground.

"Steve, that's too slow," Jenny said with sarcasm. "He's long gone."

She didn't mean it as a joke, but everyone laughed in relief. At least I hoped it was in relief and not at my expense.

"Just checking to see if I could still beat the plate to the ground.

"Congratulations," Jenny said. "As a prize, you pay the hotel two bits."

Chapter 19

Breakfast seemed tasteless. I kept going over the events of the prior evening, and I couldn't help but think that I had made a huge blunder. I had him. I might not get another chance. Every other time I had encountered the sheriff, he had been surrounded by his men. Now that I had stood up to him, he would make sure that I never had another opportunity for a one-on-one fight.

I should have killed him.

As I sipped coffee, another thought struck me. Why had he come to our picnic? Not to kill us. He still wanted our money. He couldn't have merely wanted to show off how much he knew about our activities. There had to be more. Did our altercation waylay his intended purpose? What could that purpose have been? We were armed, yet he waltzed up to us with only distant protection. He had kept his deputies out of earshot. So … the sheriff wanted to discuss something he didn't want his deputies to overhear. What?

He knew about my encounter with his deputies, knew we had bought guns and ammunition, knew we were on a picnic, knew we were shooting. Did he also know about our meeting with the tong? My telegram to the Denver Pinkerton's office? I doubted the hotel manager's daughter blabbed, so it had to be about the tong … or maybe something entirely different. If he knew we had gone to the tong, he didn't need to keep his deputies from hearing our discussion. In fact, he would want them around so he could be as intimidating as possible. What was the real purpose of our aborted meeting?

If he had a larger agenda, then it required privacy. What was he scheming for beyond the extortion? Setting us up to disappear? That would be easy. All he needed was a tragic accident. Logic said he might have wanted to further his goal of tearing la Junta Mixta into warring factions so he could live the good life without watching his backside. His greatest fear had to be the tong, because they had a brother organization in San Francisco. I thought. What was I missing? It would be very difficult to wipe out the local tong, because it was large and dispersed throughout the area. Heck, even the Del Monte hired tong laborers.

How would I do it?

I had a revelation. The sheriff might be crazy, but he wasn't stupid. He would understand the Chinese overriding loyalty to their tong. He would also fear his own men, who could move freely in San Francisco. He would least fear El Jefe and his Mexican bandits. The Mexicans might suspect a double cross, but they expected nothing less from the white man. They would be unlikely to pursue him to his home in the tony parts of a big city they didn't know.

If the tong believed they could deal with El Jefe, the sheriff could make a deal as well. Would he offer money for looking the other way? Then I had an idea. He was smart. He would offer Monterey and Santa Cruz counties to El Jefe. The Mexican bandits would be free to plunder without competition. El Jefe would become rich and powerful. I laughed to myself. In the Old World, he would be a count, in fact, a double count, because he would rule two counties. El Jefe would jump at the chance.

There was one difficulty. The sheriff had to convince El Jefe to decimate the tong.

Would the sheriff offer to help? How many men did the sheriff have? I doubted there were enough to singly take on the tong, but he could win with Mexicans at his side. The hotel manager said the whites numbered far fewer than the other two gangs in la Junta Mixta, but his men had to extend beyond deputies. The county budget would limit how many of his gang he could deputize. The sheriff would prefer to pit the Mexicans alone against the Chinese, but it made more sense to wage a combined war. He would pay off his surviving gang members and promise the Mexicans the leavings. That way, both gang elements he feared would be weakened, perhaps drastically.

How would the sheriff incite a war? Oh, crap. My meeting with the leaders of the tong worked directly into his plans. He could tell his people that the tong was separately extorting me and did not plan on sharing the payoff. A secret side deal? Then I had a new thought. I bet we hadn't succeeded in secretly sneaking out of the back of the hotel. We were followed, probably not by a deputy, but a gang member without a badge. His men would believe the sheriff's story because they had witnessed our secret rendezvous and speculated about the reason among themselves.

I had underestimated the sheriff.

I still hadn't figured out the purpose of his visit to our supper on the shore, but whatever he had in mind, it would advance his agenda of igniting an internal la Junta war.

I had another problem to figure out. The hotel manager had waylaid me on the way to the dining room to inform me that the twenty-five thousand dollars had arrived at the bank. The second twenty-five thousand for the tong would take a few more days. I didn't trust anyone in Monterey, so I gave him written instructions to withdraw the money and put it in his office safe. I also told him to keep the news between the two of us. He agreed quickly and marched off. He didn't want to be seen conversing in whispers with me.

Now what to do. Stall? Set a drop-off time with the sheriff? Should I even inform the women or keep it to myself for a day or two? I sighed. As much as I disliked William, I didn't have the right to gamble with his life. We would get him back while the promise of a larger two-hundred-and-fifty-thousand-dollar payday worked to his benefit. They would honor their side of the deal because the sheriff wanted his private extortion. Released, it might even—

"Ya look to be thinkin' hard."

The voice from behind startled the hell out of me. I whipped around in my seat to see a middle-aged man with an attractive woman. I leaped to my feet.

"Jeff, Nora, damn, am I glad to see you!" I gave them both a welcome hug, Nora with both arms, but Sharp with a single arm while we shook hands. "What are you doing here? Last I heard, you were in New Orleans."

Jeff Sharp and I had been friends since I'd made my way out west. We had ridden trail together, fought side by side, and even got married in a joint ceremony. He usually dressed like a fastidious trail hand, but today he looked like an eastern gentleman. His wife, Nora, could compete with my mother for the best-dressed Del Monte guest.

"New Orleans was gettin' old, but luckily, Joseph sent us a telegram sayin' that ya got yer dumb ass in trouble again. So we hopped a train and here we are." He looked around. "Where's Virginia?"

"Upstairs. She'll be down as soon as she gets her hair the way she wants it. Joseph telegraphed you? That means he must have received my wire. Where is he?"

"Spendin' yer money, Steve. He's in Denver assemblin' an expensive team of Pinkertons. Should be here in a day or two. Tell me, how'd ya get in trouble again? We're supposed to be quiet family men now."

I motioned them into seats, but Nora excused herself to go upstairs to see Virginia. Sharp said he was hungry. Not a surprise. He always had a big appetite. I ordered breakfast for both of us because I had barely touched my earlier meal. and it was cold. Suddenly, I was hungry. I had help, real help. A warrior who fought like a seasoned trooper. And male companionship to boot. Ever since they had grabbed William, I had been surrounded by three strong-willed women eager to get out of our predicament. Sharp would give me far more leeway in how I went about the task.

Sharp had bossed cattle drives, traveled all over the Americas as an importer-exporter, and owned some of the biggest silver mines in Nevada. We had met in Pickhandle Gulch, a Nevada mining encampment, when I had gotten on the wrong side of a competing mine owner. We had ended up becoming allies in a statewide feud. Sharp was in his fifties, but unless he had gotten soft living the easy life, he was tough as an anvil and possessed a mule-kick punch. Not a bad rifle shot either. I assumed he was still rich. He enjoyed gambling, but seldom lost, so unless his new wife had discovered imaginative ways to spend his fortune, he should still be well off.

I laughed to myself. Despite Sharp having money, I knew this breakfast would be on me. It was a game he usually won. He almost always found a way for me to pay for his food and drinks.

I had started to explain my situation, when I sensed someone at my shoulder. By Sharp's expression, I knew it wasn't Virginia. I screwed around in my chair to see Sam and Rod.

"What do you want?" I asked.

"Sheriff's gettin' jumpy. Sent us to find out when you'll be ready to complete that barter trade we discussed."

"Today."

"Today? Just like that." Sam seemed genuinely perplexed. "You're ready?"

"Found out on my way in to breakfast. Tell me when *La Virgen de Guadalupe* will be docked at the wharf." Sam started to smile, so I added, "And make sure my package is delivered intact, or we'll no longer do business." I paused for dramatic effect. "Make sure the sheriff understands that."

"You don't tell us what to do."

"I just did. Tell the sheriff that our other transaction depends on this deal going perfectly."

"What other transaction?" Rod asked.

In response, I merely stared at the two deputies.

Finally, Sam asked, "Who's yer friend?"

"Go back to your table. I'll introduce you at a more appropriate time."

"Damn it, don't tell us what to do," Sam stammered. "We tell you."

"Please return to your table," I said politely.

Sam shoulder-bumped Rod, grinning like a schoolboy. In fact, they were just boys grown large who had never matured beyond schoolyard bullies. Only now, they had badges that shielded them from repercussions for being ill-mannered brutes.

Suddenly, Sharp started laughing. "Ya take guff from these two. Come on, Steve, ya've brushed aside men twice as tough as these fools."

Sam appeared startled as he appraised Sharp. He expected a weak response from an older grandee apparently dressed for the theater. I reached out a restraining hand to Sharp, but he moved too fast for me. Before Sam could utter a phrase that would match his sneer, Sharp hit him square on the nose. Sam went down like a scarecrow whose bailing wire had been cut. I shoved my chair back into Rod and spun into a standing position before he could react to his partner being knocked to the floor. Rod didn't move after he saw my gun-filled hand.

"Pick up Sam and go back to your table," I said evenly.

"You think you can get away with this?" Rod said. "We're the law."

"Then ya shoulda said so," Sharp said. He leaned down and helped Sam to his feet. "Don't like to ruffle the feathers of the law. Thought ya were just regular dummies."

"What? What did ya say?" Sam exclaimed, holding his nose. "Damn it, yer under arrest."

"Better get more deputies," Sharp said with a grin.

Sam thought about going for his gun, but Sharp stepped right up to him and shook his finger in a tsk-tsk motion. Sam's expressions went all over the map. Anger, confusion, unease, and whatever else cycled through his limited intellect. He wanted to arrest this troublesome city dweller, but Sharp showed no fear of him. Why? There was something he didn't understand.

Sam surrendered.

Without further comment, Sam and Rod returned to their table.

I explained in a low voice, "Jenny is with us, along with her new husband. In truth, he's missing. The sheriff and his deputies are part of a gang that abducted her husband for ransom. We've been tiptoeing around these men so they wouldn't hurt William." I saw confusion on Sharp's face. "That's Jenny's husband."

"Damn, I shoulda waited until I knew more. Instead, I blundered in like normal." Sharp grinned. "Got any more apple carts around?"

"A few." I said, and then took fifteen minutes to explain everything.

When we had finished eating, we sipped coffee until Virginia and Nora joined us. Virginia was obviously thrilled to see Nora. She probably also appreciated seeing Sharp, but her eyes lit up with excitement as she chatted with her friend. They laughed, touched hands, and frequently talked simultaneously. Nora went on and on about Jeffie, her husband's namesake, claiming he was the cutest child in all of Christendom.

During a break in their conversation, I gave Nora a highly abridged version of our predicament.

At the end, Nora said, "As you know, I'm not fond of Joseph McAllen, but in this case, I hope he hurries."

"As do we," Virginia said.

We all glanced at the door, but McAllen hadn't magically appeared simply because we had wished it.

When we returned our attention to the table, Sharp glanced at the deputies and leaned in close to me. "This sounds serious."

"It is. The sheriff's cunning and greedy. A bad combination. They're holding one of our party hostage, and the three gangs are working together to threaten my family's well-being. Worse—" I looked Sharp in the eye. "After I pay, I don't believe the sheriff will bid us adieu."

"Glad ya see it as it is." Sharp leaned in close. "Steve, ya showed yer hand. He knows once yer family's safe, ya'll come after him."

"So what do we do?"

"First, we wait for Joseph … then fight our way out of this."

Chapter 20

Sharp had asked about his namesake, so while the women continued to chat, we returned to our suite. Jeff and Jeffie soon became best friends. Sharp appeared to be as natural a charmer with children as he was with women. I didn't ask Sharp if he intended to have kids, because the answer might be that Nora was too old. The thought made me sad. They had fallen in love young, but the currents of life had swept them in different directions until recently. Now they were together at long last, but starting a family in your fifties posed serious hazards for the woman. Sharp wouldn't risk losing her again.

After the three of us had played for a while, I asked Juanita to take charge of my son again so Jeff and I could make a courtesy visit to Jenny's suite. Jenny ran hot and cold with me and despised Joseph McAllen, but she had a soft spot for Sharp. As a result, our visit went well. She was as thrilled as I that we had another competent fighter on our side. When I told her that we would soon have the ransom money downstairs in the manager's office, her reaction was subdued. I didn't believe that Mother had totally convinced her that she needed William at her side to run her empire. When we relayed our encounter with Sam and Rod, she got excited and said she wished she had been there to see it. Jenny always liked a good fight, especially when she engineered it.

Next, we visited my mother, who was less than gracious. Sharp's charm worked only occasionally with her, and she remained peeved that I hadn't killed the sheriff the night before. Despite professing to be happy that Sharp had arrived to offer help, she uncharacteristically seemed fatalistic about our predicament. Her entire trip was not anywhere near what she had envisioned. After half an hour, she succumbed somewhat to Sharp's magic, but I knew she found him far too rough around the edges for genuine friendship.

When we returned to my sitting room, Sharp asked, "After our encounter, why didn't one of those deputies go get the sheriff?"

"Same reason they didn't arrest us. They want our money. After they get it, they'll make us regret we ever gave them a hard time. Besides, the sheriff's got a red-hot temper. They'll tell him, but they need time to frame it just right so he doesn't go off half-cocked."

"What will this phony lawman do when he finds out?"

I thought. "The first thing he'll do is size you up. Let's tell him you're newly rich and came here on a whim because I wrote we were planning a holiday at one of the best resorts in the country. We can say you were a boxer a long time ago and leave unmentioned your skill with a rifle." I paused for a moment. "Be your normal gruff self. I think we're beyond playing possum. Let's push back, but not too aggressively. We'll be safe enough until we deliver over the extortion money."

Sharp thought. "That means we've got three or four days to plot our assault ... or escape. Ya are gettin' the money, ain't ya?"

I shrugged. "I have to pay the ransom of course, and I want to have the cash I promised the tong. That's for sure. As for the rest ... well, I'm pretending to gather up the whole quarter million, but I don't intend to pay. In fact, I'm sure paying would be our death warrant." I thought some more. "The immediate need is to get William back safe. Once we're all together again, we have more options."

"He handy in a fight?" Sharp asked.

"Opposite. I'd choose any of the women over him."

"Damn. That don't bode well for his marriage. Jenny's a handful for anyone. She'll hog-tie a milksop."

"I suspect he's starting to figure that out, but my bet is that they can make it work. Imagine Jenny married to a strong-willed man."

Sharp laughed. "Yep, got a point there all right."

To get Sharp's perspective, I explained how I was supposed to deliver the money and said I believed William would be set free, because previous abductees had been released, and the sheriff wanted the bigger payoff.

Sharp nodded agreement, then asked, "Steve. Ya were deep in thought when Nora an' I arrived. Ya always gotta plan. What is it?"

"Not so much a plan as a strategy. And I'm losing confidence it'll work."

"Tell me anyway," Sharp said.

I told him.

I told him all of it.

"Do ya trust the tong?" Sharp asked.

"Not sure. Mother says if they give their word, they're good for it as long as it doesn't jeopardize their tong. I need to meet with them again. Measure their commitment." I shook my head. "I want to turn the tong against the sheriff's men. I suspect the sheriff wants to turn his men against the tong. Both the sheriff and I want El Jefe to stay out of the fight." I laughed. "We both have the same strategy, but for different reasons. Gets confusing."

"Too confusin'," Sharp said with finality. "To my way of thinkin', simple's best. El Jefe an' his men have been here the longest. Put yerself in El Jefe's boots. The Mexicans feel entitled. This was their land. They want their territory back. That's the sheriff's promise. A few thousand ain't gonna satisfy them. Steve, it doesn't matter why they don't fight, just so they don't. An' they won't. Whether due to your bribe or the sheriff's promise, the Mexicans will sit around watchin' the carnage as they laugh into their tequila. So that leaves the other two gangs in la Junta. With the right push, the Chinese an' whites will fight it out to the death. Yer goal's to survive until that war ends." He paused dramatically. "That's the hard part, 'cuz it could take a while. A long while."

"What are you suggesting?" I asked.

"Ya can't dictate why they're fightin' ... but ya might control the start of this war."

I had an inkling of where Sharp was going. "You think I should start it soon ... before McAllen arrives, not after."

"Not just before. Now." He smiled. "Right now."

I thought about his idea, then I shook my head.

"No, not right now. We have something that needs to be done first."

Chapter 21

Sharp brought clarity to my strategy. A few days of delay presented a false hope. We would just continue to spar with the sheriff and his deputies. At the end, they would take our money and our lives. Joseph McAllen's arrival might be a reason to delay, but McAllen's army didn't matter until we got into the fight. Getting lead and blades flying inside the Junta could whittle down the numbers before McAllen showed up.

But there was a prerequisite to starting a la Junta Mixta revolution. We needed to get William back. We had the ransom cash, so we should be able to get the job done in short order. With this is mind, I took a cabriolet to the sheriff's office. Alone. I tend to hold my cards close to my vest and didn't want to flaunt an asset as important as Sharp.

I asked the cabriolet driver to wait outside and stepped across the boardwalk and into the office. The sheriff stood at the window, obviously observing my arrival. No deputies were in sight.

"Good morning, Sheriff. Have you seen Sam and Rod?"

"No. They're assigned to watch the Del Monte." He turned from looking out the window. "What do you want?"

"They were supposed to inform you that we have the ransom money. I told them to tell you right away. We want to get this done and return William to his wife."

He stared at me for a long moment. "What about the other issue?"

"That will take at least four more days. That's a much larger amount."

"Then we'll wait. I want both done at once. Go back to your fancy hotel and don't bother me until you have all the money. Now git. I have other concerns."

"No. We exchange the ransom for William, and he's returned safe and sound. Otherwise, we'll assume you're untrustworthy … and you'll get nothing. Not the ransom, not the extortion."

The sheriff took a step toward me. "You don't make the rules."

"I made that one." When he didn't respond, I added, "You need to prove we can trust you."

His smile showed confidence. "All right, you can have that daisy back. Good riddance. We'll do it today. But understand this: If you try to leave town, I'll know, and one of the people in your party will die. No further questions. No negotiations. Just bam! Dead. And it will probably be one of the women. Understand?"

I was so angry, I couldn't trust myself to speak, so I just nodded.

The sheriff gave me an appraising look and then said, "You know how to deliver the money?"

"Throw it onto the deck of *La Virgen de Guadalupe*," I answered.

"Be sure you throw it. Don't step one foot onto that boat. Just toss the bag on board, turn around, and walk away. Do you understand?"

"No, I don't understand. How do we get William? Will he be at the wharf? How will the exchange be made?"

"Don't worry, he'll wander into the hotel within an hour of your delivering the money. Assuming it's all there. The ship will sail immediately, and once at sea, they'll count the money. If it's all there, they'll signal with Marryat flags, and we'll let your tedious friend go."

For war ships, Marryat signal flags had been supplanted over twenty years ago by the International Code of Signals, but they were still used by small commercial boats. Clever. The accomplices got to safely count the money off the coast, run up a signal flag, and then sail to an unknown port. Even if I had found law enforcement willing to get involved, they would be hard-pressed to track these criminals. I should have investigated the prior abductions at the Del Monte. If I had, I might have learned the ransom technique and hired a boat to follow the abductors.

"When?" I asked.

"In two hours. You come alone."

I shook my head. "I'll come with a guard to help protect the money. I heard there are bad people down by the wharf. It would ruin everything if I were to get robbed."

"Bullshit ... and you know it. Nobody robs anyone without my permission. You and your money will be safe."

I did know it, so I acquiesced. "I'll come alone, but I'll consider any trouble to mean you're not trustworthy. Keep me safe. It's worth a quarter million dollars to you."

The sheriff turned red and compressed his lips in a straight line.

"Get out!" he exclaimed. As I retreated out the door, he added, "Better hurry. If you're late, I'll consider you untrustworthy."

I allowed him to have the last word.

Chapter 22

I stepped out of my cabriolet at the entry to the wharf because I didn't know the berth location for *La Virgen de Guadalupe*. The harbor was full and brimming with activity. Some boats bobbed offshore, while others were moored along a series of docks that stretched into the harbor. The wharf was a babel of male voices. Men laughed and jostled each other as they yelled greetings and good-natured insults. Many of the boats were unloading their catch. Fishermen and stevedores were cheerful, boisterous, and moving with purpose. Gulls squawked at the food but only tentatively approached the tubs of squirming fish. The bolder pelicans came up on the dock and lunged toward the fish whenever they saw an opening. Occasionally, they would get a reward for their audaciousness, but more often a kick in their direction would cause them to fly away.

Fishing may have been good, but the catch wasn't nearly as valuable as the one I was carrying in a threadbare carpetbag. About halfway through the harbor, I spotted a steam-powered boat tied up at the far end of a dock. I saw vapor pouring from her stack, which meant she was ready to cast off. A portrait of the Virgin of Guadalupe painted on the side of the wheelhouse told me I'd found the boat I was looking for. The weather-beaten image had faded but remained recognizable, even from a distance. The figure stood erect on top of a crescent moon, her hands joined in prayer. Although the colors had been washed out by sun and wind, I could still make out the pink of her robe and the blue-green of her shawl. The full-length representation was well-known to anyone familiar with Mexican culture.

I looked around. Sure enough, I spotted several Chinese who were undoubtedly lookouts for the tong. One of them nodded in the direction of the ship. Obviously, they had been waiting for me.

As I walked the length of the dock, I wondered about the difference between a boat and a ship. I thought of ships as big and boats as small. *La Virgen de Guadalupe* appeared to be in between. My guess was that she was about fifty feet. She certainly could handle a carpetbag of money. That thought brought a different observation to mind. *La Virgen de Guadalupe* had been picked for speed, not for size. She had a head of steam and could probably outrun anything I could have hired to chase her. The sheriff had thought this out. I stopped walking and examined the boat that wanted to be a ship. After more thought, I decided to meet El Jefe. I was willing to bet that he supplemented his banditry with a little smuggling on the side.

As I approached the end of the dock, I inspected the back of the boat. Sure enough, "La Virgen de Guadalupe" had been painted across the stern. The boat showed wear, but she was scrubbed clean and tidy. Although at least a small crew must have been on board, I spotted no one. I waited a second, but no one showed, so I tossed the carpetbag into the center of the aft deck. It landed with a heavy thud. Without warning, the stern sat down in the water, and *La Virgen de Guadalupe* sailed away with surprising speed. Soon she was hundreds of yards away from the dock and swiftly moving out to open sea. Damn, I hadn't noticed that the boat wasn't tied up. Someone in the wheelhouse had been using steam power to expertly keep the ship aligned with the dock. A fast boat and a skilled pilot. Yes, El Jefe probably did well transporting contraband between Mexico and the United States.

When I turned back toward shore, a slight Chinese man blocked my path up the dock. It suddenly occurred to me that the sheriff had guaranteed my safety only until I delivered the money. I knew about tong members' prowess with knives and hands, so I stopped my approach twenty feet from the man.

The Chinese smiled. "No worry, Mister. I not harm you." He spread his arms wide. "How could little man hurt big man like you?"

"Without my even knowing I was hurt until blood gushed, I suppose."

His smile turned genuine. "You know Chinese tong. Good." He nodded. "Mutual respect good. I came to tell you that your friend will be delivered to hotel soon."

"I was told within an hour of *La Virgen de Guadalupe* sailing."

He made an exaggerated shrug with palms up. "An hour, maybe two. We see. First must verify cargo."

I pulled out my watch and made a point of studying it. "One hour ... or I will return angry."

"What you do with anger? Can it kill dozens?"

"Probably not, but I *can* kill you. Now please turn around and walk away from me."

He smiled with apparent humor and then slowly turned and walked away. I followed, staying twenty feet behind. When we reached the end of the dock, the Chinese bowed and waved his arm in a broad arc, a welcoming gesture that signaled I was free to proceed to wherever I wanted.

I stepped into the street and hailed a cabriolet. When it stopped, I noticed the driver was Chinese. I looked back at the man I had just been conversing with, and he nodded that I should take the buggy. Was this a trap? I didn't know, but if they wanted to do me harm, I suspected it would have already happened. I climbed in and jostled my gun so it was within easy reach. Without a word between us, the driver sped off in the direction of the Hotel Del Monte.

When we arrived at the resort, the driver accepted his fare and tip before saying, "Wait in lobby. Few minutes only."

With an air snap of his whip, he was gone.

As I entered the lobby, I scanned the large well-appointed room for Sam and Rod. Neither was in sight. I spotted none of the people in my party either, so I went into the bar and ordered a beer. When it came, I took the glass and carried it to the main lobby, choosing a corner wingback chair and making myself comfortable. I didn't need to wait long. In less than an hour, William walked into the lobby, looking none the worse for wear. Puzzled, I stood to greet him and saw that he had all ten of his fingers. I almost laughed. They had used someone else's finger with his wedding ring.

I walked up, gripped him around the shoulder, and clapped his back. "Welcome back," I said.

"What the hell took so long? I thought I would die from that awful food. Did you know Chinese chop up chickens with the bones still in them? Beastly."

I almost hit him right there but restrained myself. "Did they take your wedding ring?"

He looked at his hand. "Oh, yes, they did. Told me they were going to put it on the finger of a corpse. For some reason, my captors thought that was funny, so they shared it with me."

"They delivered the finger in a tobacco tin with the ransom note. They wanted us to believe they would go to any length to get paid." I patted him on the shoulder. "You can pick up your ring in my room."

"Heavens, I'll never wear it until it has been thoroughly cleaned by an expert jeweler. Just thinking about it on a dead finger gives me the shivers."

"Just be glad it wasn't one of your fingers."

"I am. That would have hurt like hell." He literally quivered "But in truth, they were decent enough blokes. Chinese, but decent enough at that. Love to gamble, though. Reckless gamblers, if you ask me. Still, all in all, it was mostly just rotten food and isolation." He grinned conspiratorially. "Tell me, how much did I fetch?"

"How much did you fetch?" I asked, incredulous.

"Yes. How much was the ransom? They said their previous record was twenty thousand. I bet I beat that hands down."

I wanted to know if they had bashed him on the head, but instead asked, "Where did they keep you?"

"Some room down by the ocean. Couldn't see out, but I could smell fish and sea air. Seagulls woke me in the mornings. It wasn't bad. Bed, chair, chamber pot, and a tattered Bible. Didn't read much. Had enough of the Bible as a kid. We played a lot of whist. I won over six dollars at a nickel a point." He grinned. "Pretty good, huh?"

I was flabbergasted. "You sound like you enjoyed captivity!"

"Not at all. I'd rather have been with Jenny. I missed that. Hey, you know how it can be without ... " He let his voice trail off and winked. "But it wasn't terrible. That is, after I got over the fear that they would kill me. I learned to make the most of it. My guards were supposed to be outside my door, but I convinced them they could do their job while we played cards. Just like our all-night games at Harvard, only for lower stakes. They even shared beer with me occasionally."

"Maybe we should've traded places," I said, thinking about our troubles dealing with la Junta Mixta.

"No, Steve." He patted me on the back. "This was no honeymoon. Listen, I'm just making it sound easy. Stiff upper lip, as the British say. It wasn't all card games and beer. The bed was lumpy, and they forgot to empty my chamber pot on occasion. I doubt you could have handled it. It took guts and finesse for me to win over my jailers." Now he slapped me on the back and laughed. "It wasn't nearly as simple as I made it sound."

I wanted to rearrange his smug face but instead said, "Let's get upstairs. There are people who will be pleased to see that you're free."

"I wasn't free, was I? Come on, tell me. How much did I command in ransom?"

"Why? Do you want to brag to your fraternity buddies?"

"Of course. What are fraternity brothers for? Now quit teasing. How much?"

"Twenty-five thousand."

"That's all?" He appeared crestfallen.

"That was quite enough. One-third of the money was mine. A thank-you would be appreciated."

"Really? You put up some of the money? I'm flattered." He smiled broadly. "I didn't think you liked me."

"I don't," I said more forcibly than I'd intended.

"Oh, misery me. Don't worry, you'll come to like me soon enough. Jenny did, and she couldn't stand me at first. And listen, I don't hold grudges, especially not with family." He leaned his head near my ear and stage whispered, "In truth, I'm not too fond of you either."

"That's a relief," I answered, letting him figure out what part of his comment I meant. "Let's get upstairs. Your wife has been at wit's end about you."

"Hardly sleeps, cries all day?" He slapped me on the back yet again. "Women. You can't please them when you're around, and you can't please them when you're away. Good thing she's rich, or I might be like you, heading off into the Wild West looking for adventure."

As we climbed the stairs, my pseudo brother-in-law added, "In case you didn't notice, I never thanked you. Quite purposefully, I might add."

Chapter 23

When I knocked on Jenny's door, she yelled to come in. I was thrilled that she was in her room, and I wouldn't have to endure a group reunion. At least not yet. I needed a respite from Mr. Harvard Goodfellow. I nodded toward the door and walked away before William could invite me to stay.

In my suite, I found Sharp, Nora, Virginia, and Jeffie. Jeffie seemed intent on boisterously throwing every one of his toys to another part of the room.

"Where's Mother?" I asked.

"Shopping," Virginia answered. "She's looking for toys for Jeffie."

I inspected the toy-strewn floor. "She was bored, I assume."

Sharp chuckled. "She probably needed a break from my relentless charm."

"Come on, Jeff," Virginia said, "Mrs. Dancy adores you."

"She thinks I'm a bad influence on her son is what she thinks."

"Well, she can't blame you for this donnybrook," I said. "When this kicked off, you were a thousand miles away in New Orleans."

"She believes I can curse ya from afar."

"That you can," I said. "You have a knack for profanity."

Everyone politely chuckled, then looked at me with serious intent.

I sighed. "William has returned. None the worse for wear. Even sporting ten whole fingers, I might add. The one they sent to us was from a corpse. He and his captors had a laugh over that one. Anyway, William had a grand 'ol time and took his captors for over six dollars at whist." I pulled over a ladder-back chair and sat. "He's currently with Jenny."

"Ya don't sound thrilled to see him back," Sharp said, sounding genuinely perplexed.

"He's okay in small doses. The question is, what do we do now?"

Sharp grinned. "Start a war."

"Agreed." I stood. "Jeff, let's take this downstairs and allow the reunion to commence without our sour faces."

With no objection, we left the women and went down to the bar to order strong drinks to bolster strong conversation. We needed to figure out how to get this gang war going. The first step would be to ask Mother to expedite Max Lee's release. Next, we would go to the docks to see the tong leaders again. Nelson would need to set up another meeting. Next, a visit to the sheriff. Last, I convinced Sharp we should visit El Jefe so we would know what kind of man we were dealing with.

We finished our planning, and within an hour, Nelson had set a meeting with the tong. Sharp and I rented a cabriolet to take us to that filthy alleyway.

As we jostled along, I asked Sharp, "Have you dealt with Chinese before?"

"Many times, but never with a tong. I kept those gangsters away from my laborers."

"Maybe we should have brought my mother. She seems to have had extensive experience with bad elements within the New York Chinese community."

"Not until she completes her side of the bargain," Sharp said. "She needs to get Mack Lee released, or that'll be the tong's sole focus. At the moment, she's a distraction."

That made sense, but I suspected Mother's presence at yesterday's meeting had tempered ill will. The Chinese did not trust white men. Mexicans did not trust whites or Chinese. And nobody trusted a corrupt sheriff. A lot of hostility around. All we had to do was ignite it into a shooting war.

In ten minutes, we rapped on the tin door to the tong shed.

From inside, we heard the simple command, "Come."

The shed was as dark, dank, and shabby as on the previous day. The same three slightly built gentlemen sat on the same backless stools. They waved us to two facing stools.

Before our butts hit the seat, the leader asked Sharp, "Who are you?"

"*Nín hǎo*," Sharp said. "Jeff Sharp ... *Péngyǒu*."

The tong leader harrumphed, then turned to me. "Why you need friend? You break our deal?"

"No, sir. I came because deputies confronted us this morning. I needed to talk to you, and I feel better traveling the city with Mr. Sharp at my side."

The tong leader turned back to Sharp. "Please, speak English. Your Chinese hurts."

Sharp laughed pleasantly. "Thank ya. I'm flat out of Chinese words."

I thought I detected a wisp of a smile on the leader's face. But it quickly faded, and he stated, "Lee still in custody."

"Yes, he is," I agreed. "Telegrams have been sent. These things take time."

"You not have time."

I paused dramatically. "Nor do you."

The tong leader didn't question further. He just sat there patiently, more patiently than me, so I added, "We're here to warn you. The sheriff knows you intend a double cross."

Not the slightest flinch. "How he know?" Then he added, "How you know what sheriff know?"

"His deputies. He sent them to question us. Somehow he knew about our visit yesterday."

"He follow you yesterday," he stated. It wasn't a question.

"No. I believe he bought one of your men. He knew the details about our arrangement. Things said inside this room."

"Cannot be. No one goes against tong. No one. Penalty severe."

"Perhaps." I looked between the three men. "Did you talk about our arrangement with anyone outside this room?"

"No," the leader said firmly.

"Then if someone told the sheriff ..." I waved my finger at the three Chinese, "it was one of you."

"Or your mother," the leader said shortly.

"Or my mother ... but neither of us benefit from telling the sheriff. Our agreement can get us out of our predicament."

I let that sink in before adding, "The sheriff knows the details, so it was one of you three. Either one of you told a conduit to the sheriff, or you blabbed to someone who did." I paused. "I'll let you sort that out. I'm here to warn you that the deputies said your fishermen are not all safe."

The leader appeared puzzled. "What he say ... exactly?"

"He said, 'We know your deal with the tong. They can't handle El Jefe, and they won't catch our men unawares. The Junta must remain united, so the tong must pay a price for their treason. Tomorrow, one of their fishermen will not return to the harbor.' Or ... something close to that."

One of the flanking Chinese asked, "Why attack fishermen? They are laborers."

The leader mused, "Because he isolated with white man and unskilled in fighting. To embarrass us. We no protect our brothers."

We sat quiet for almost a minute.

"Thank you," the leader said.

"Do we still have a deal?" I asked.

"Meeting over. Please leave."

"Answer my question, and I'll leave."

A staring contest ensued.

After I lost our little competition, I said, "We warned you. We could have kept quiet. Even if you avoid the sheriff's wrath this time, you won't forever. If you bring this to a head now, we're here to help." I shrugged. "Later, maybe not." I waited for a response. When none came, I added, "If we leave without a positive answer to my question, my mother will not get Max Lee released."

I stood, and Sharp followed my lead.

As we turned for the door, the tong leader said, "We have deal. Deal is you get Lee released. If not, you break deal. Understand?"

"Understood."

We left and walked the ten minutes to the sheriff's office. Along the way, Sharp told me about his experience with tongs and mentioned that those frail-looking men were quite dangerous. That was why he kept tongs away from his Chinese mine workers. Not for his own safety, which would have been secure if he didn't abuse a Chinese, but for the safety of his white miners. If any of them verbally or physically assaulted a Chinese, the tong would take retribution. If the tong wanted to set an example, they might break an arm, gouge an eye, or merely break a finger. He said those little men could physically punish burly offenders in the blink of an eye. They could even beat a man to death through rapid kicks and punches. They were also skilled with knives, poisons, and potions, but preferred to pummel their enemies. If they wanted to send a message but remain faceless, the offending miner might puke until his stomach was empty. On occasion, a wrongdoer would die in his sleep or simply disappear, but only rarely, because the tong wanted it known that whites should not mess with the people under their protection.

Sharp said he had witnessed feuds between Chinese and whites. When a tong fulfilled their obligation to protect members of their gang, white miners often escalated the dispute. The spiraling conflict quickly became a bloodbath. Whites eventually won, but only because of overwhelming numbers, not superior weapons or skill. Sharp felt that the safest way to avoid conflict was keeping the tongs away from his workers and telling his miners that if anyone initiated a fight with any person under his employ, they would be immediately dismissed.

Sharp walked in silence the remaining distance to the sheriff's office.

With a hand on the doorknob, he added, "Tongs can put on the appearance of bein' harmless, but never forget, they are ruthless gang lords who kill their enemies."

Chapter 24

When we opened the door, the sheriff and two deputies immediately scattered to opposite corners of the room, hands resting on guns. Nobody drew. Sharp and I calmly stood shoulder to shoulder and held our hands head high, palms out, and away from our bodies. Sharp was unarmed, but I wore my Colt.

Looking at Sharp, the sheriff demanded, "Is this the man?"

"Yep, that's him," Sam answered.

"You're under arrest," the sheriff said. "You going to give us trouble?"

"No, sir. We came to help ya," Sharp answered.

"Help? Who the hell are you?"

"Name's Jeff Sharp. Friend of Steve, here. My wife an' I came to Monterey to enjoy a holiday with the Dancys, but he told me 'bout his troubles. Damn, sounds like a pretty lousy holiday."

"Fella, you'll holiday in my jail. You punched an officer of the law."

Sharp smiled. "Hell, ya can't hold that against me. I didn't know they were law. Look like a couple of ill-bred ruffians with no manners. 'Sides, if they can't take a punch, ya need tougher men."

Sam stepped forward. "Want to try again?"

"Naw, no grudge. Just try to be more polite next time."

Sam's head snapped back. "Hey, I'm not—"

This was not going in the direction we needed, so I interrupted, "Sheriff, we have information for you. I apologize for the unfortunate incident, but this is important. We just returned from—"

He pointed at me. "You bludgeoned my deputies," then swung his finger to point at Sharp, "and your friend here waltzes into town and slugs Sam." He took a step toward Sharp. "I don't know how things work where you come from, but you can't treat the law like that in this town." He paced in front of us, thinking hard. "I need Mr. Dancy free to do my bidding, but this jerk is going into one of my cells. Right now! No more of this disrespect."

Sharp said, "Meant no disrespect, Sheriff." He turned to face Sam square. "I apologize, sir. I just had an argument with my wife before ya came along. I needed to release my anger, an' ya presented a handy target. Nothin' personal. Ya shouldn't have come over an' acted pushy. I just kinda blew up. Can't we—"

"Shut up!" the sheriff screamed. "Rod, put this man in cell one."

"Just a second, Sheriff," I said. "You need to hear what we have to say first."

"You tell me … he can rot."

"Can't we just settle for a fine?" Sharp asked. "I'll also pay yer deputy a double eagle."

"You can't afford the fine for hitting one of my deputies," the sheriff said.

"Sure, I can," Sharp chuckled "What can it be? Ten bucks? I'll pay it right here."

"Ten thousand won't keep you out of this cell. The only question that remains is whether you go willingly or resist arrest." The sheriff stepped forward, hand still on gun. "Please resist."

"That's not the only question," I said. "Do you want to know about a budding revolt in la Junta or not?"

The sheriff looked at me. "Let me guess. If I arrest your friend, you won't tell me. Let me save you the breath." His face contorted into a mocking sneer. "If you won't tell me, I'll beat it out of him once he's in my cell. And I'll beat on you too. I'll rough you up so hard, you'll never allow any of your friends to touch one of my boys again."

Sharp's expression turned from jovial to hard. "Ya got that right, Sheriff. Yer deputies are boys. No man would let himself get punched to the ground an' then slink away to his boss, cryin' for protection."

What was Sharp doing? I kept trying to smooth things out, and he kept throwing kerosene on the fire. What was he thinking? Then I remembered that Sharp knew men and dangerous situations. He didn't fly off the handle for no reason. He had a purpose behind pissing off the sheriff. I thought quick. Why didn't he believe the sheriff would lock him up? Then I had it. Because Jeff would blab to his deputies about the extortion game the sheriff was playing with us.

I said, "Go ahead. You can lock him up, and you can beat him, but he's strong, and he won't break easy." I shrugged. "If he does, you're right, he'll tell everything. Everything we learned about a la Junta insurrection ... and everything about my personal problems raising cash."

The deputies looked curious, and the sheriff miffed. Obviously, the deputies were suspicious that something was being kept from them.

"Sheriff," I said, "assess a fine, and we'll tell you what we know. You get the information right now, in time to do something about it. Additionally, Jeff won't need to make up conspiracies to stop the beatings." I waited a beat. "How about it?"

The sheriff relented. "Give Sam that double eagle, and we'll call it square."

Sharp pulled the gold coin out of his pocket and flipped it to Sam, who caught it and examined it to make sure it was real. That was probably a month's wages for Sam. Then I remembered that Sam made most of his money from criminal enterprises. Evidently, the sheriff wasn't overly generous, because Sam shoved the coin deep into his pocket so it wouldn't get lost.

Everyone stared at each other until the sheriff said, "If I hear guff from either of you again, I will kill Mr. Sharp. No questions, no debate, no buying your way out. Understood?"

Sharp nodded.

I said "Agreed."

Sharp chuckled. "Steve, yer pretty free an' easy barterin' my life."

"I'll behave," I said with a smile. "It's all up to you."

"You boys done ribbing each other?" the sheriff asked.

We both nodded.

"Okay, then. Sam, Rod, go get yourselves a drink. I'll take care of these two."

"Sheriff, you sure?" Rod asked, appearing confused.

"I want to hear about this supposed rebellion alone. If there's anything to it, I'll tell you. I won't sow doubts and rumors about la Junta throughout my organization."

"Ya think these assholes are bullshittin'?" Sam asked.

"They haven't told the truth yet. Now go have that drink or go clean the chamber pots in the cells. Your choice."

That got them out of the office but further raised their suspicions that the sheriff was working his own hustle.

After his deputies left, the sheriff stood arms akimbo and said, "Out with it ... and it better be good."

I hesitated only a second. "The tong approached me. They said they could help me get out of my troubles with you. In exchange for a special favor and money to bribe El Jefe, they would ambush a few of your men. Highwaymen. Further, the Chinese and Mexicans would stay out of any fight between us. They claimed you have only a few men, and after they pick off a couple, I might stand a chance."

"What favor?" the sheriff demanded.

"My mother was supposed to free a brother tong member jailed in New York City."

"Can she?"

"Yes. She's sent telegrams."

He nodded that he already knew that, but I wondered if prior to this conversation, he had connected her telegrams to the local tong.

"So you conspired against me?"

I hesitated a long moment this time, but when the sheriff said nothing more, I did my best to appear contrite. "At first, I accepted." I held up the flat of my hand. "Hold on, Sheriff, don't get riled. This morning I went to their tin hovel to renege." I grimaced. "They threatened my family in New York unless my mother kept her word, but said they would release us from our local obligations. They would let that go because they found another way to get you out of the way. Evidently, a sister tong in San Francisco has agreed to help fight you. Here ... and in San Francisco. They claim to have already sealed a deal with El Jefe and with fresh troops from up north. They bragged that the tong would soon control Monterey Bay."

The sheriff paced in silence for nearly a full minute.

"Anything else?" he asked.

"I believe they've been communicating with their tong brethren using Chinese coolies on fishing boats."

He whirled on me. "They told you that?"

"No. Of course not. My mother knows enough Chinese to understand the gist of a conversation. She overheard two hotel laundresses talk about getting a private message to a relative in San Francisco. One of them said there was an underground courier who works on a fishing boat. He carries messages between tongs, and for a price, he'll relay messages for ordinary Chinese. At today's meeting, I was told an agreement between the tongs would occur tomorrow." I shrugged. "On the walk here, I put it together."

"You guessed."

Now I smiled. "You're right, I guessed. I don't actually know. But it makes sense. The tong doesn't trust whites, not even the post service. It makes sense that they would use the fishing trawlers to deliver messages between here and San Francisco."

"And you believe that if this agreement doesn't reach San Francisco, the deal will be off."

"Probably delayed. But that's all we need to get our business concluded."

He shook his head. "You're wrong. You don't know the Chinese. They make deals verbally."

"Verbally? From over a hundred miles apart? They have to send messages … or … perhaps the courier delivers verbal messages."

The sheriff nodded thoughtfully. I had mentioned this last part as if it had just occurred to me. I needed the sheriff to believe that getting rid of the courier delayed or eliminated the threat. The need to find a piece of paper would complicate my plan.

Almost musing, he said, "There's only one fishing boat that sails from here and regularly sells its catch at the San Francisco wharf."

He paced some more, so I acted contrite.

"Sheriff, I apologize for speaking to the tong. You need to understand, I was desperate. I am desperate. I can't come up with your money as fast as you want. Selling stock isn't enough. I need to sell real estate, which means lawyers and banks. I can pay, but I need another week."

He whirled on me. "No! No more time. Can't you see this whole situation is heating up? If I move fast, I can get it done before anyone figures it out. Now it seems I have less time than I thought." He gave me a stern look. "Borrow on your real estate. Or get it from your mother. Or that pretty young thing in your party. I understand she owns most of Nevada."

I shook my head, looking forlorn. "Real estate as well. Both. Please, just a few more days."

He paced again, then whirled on us. "Day after tomorrow, you give me hard proof you're doing everything in your power to get me my money. Proof! Return telegrams. Bank balances. Whatever you got. I'll let you know after I look at it whether you can have more time. Understood?"

"Yes, sir."

I gave Sharp a pitiful look that I hope conveyed my desperation to the sheriff.

"Now get out of here," he said.

"One more thing," I said hesitantly. "If the tong has full control of Monterey and is tightly connected to the San Francisco tong, it will make San Francisco unsafe for you."

He stopped pacing and looked at me with curiosity. "Why did you say that?"

"Just a thought I had."

"A thought or a threat?"

"I wouldn't be telling you all of this if I meant it as a threat." He remained perplexed, so I added, "I hope my warnings are appreciated. I hope you take them into account."

"Into account for what?" he asked.

"When you examine my honest effort to raise the cash." I hoped my expression appeared downtrodden. "Sheriff, I need more time."

"I told you, day after tomorrow. I'll decide then. Now get out ... or by God, I'll kill you where you stand."

We left. My head hung low.

As we walked to our hotel, I asked Sharp, "What do you think?"

"He swallowed it whole. Maybe ya shoulda been a thespian."

"No thanks. Thespians are empty headed. That's why it's dangerous for them to speak without a script."

"He's going to murder all the coolies on that boat," Sharp said.

"I know." I walked a few steps before adding, "When you start a war, people die."

"Innocent people," Sharp said dejectedly.

"Not completely innocent. They wouldn't be trusted couriers if they weren't deep in the tong."

Sharp stopped walking and turned me by the shoulder. "Steve, you made up that whole story. Don't go believin' yer own lies. It's a good plan … for us, not the coolies."

"I didn't make it up. I surmised it. In my first meeting with the tong, the leader told me that they get regular reports of everything that happens in San Francisco. For instance, they knew about the sheriff's big house. They said they'd know if he ran away to live there, and if he did, the Hip Sing would kill him after they got the money back. Later, I learned that the sheriff has corrupted both telegraph operations in town. Think about it. There's no other way for San Francisco news to clandestinely get down here. The fishing boat coolies must be couriers."

Sharp did think about it. "Yer right, I can't think of another way. Still … I feel sorry to think we caused people to die."

"Thanks for saying we, but it's my plan. I carry the responsibility. But … it's not heavy. This is an outlaw gang, and they were the ones who made decisions that forced me to put them in harm's way."

Sharp appeared less than convinced. As we resumed our walk, he kicked a rock down the street.

In a low voice, he said, "It's a dirty piece of work. I hope it doesn't get any nastier."

Chapter 25

We found a quiet café to discuss our next actions. After ordering coffee, we evaluated the options. Either the sheriff would succeed in killing the fishing boat coolies, or the forewarned tong would kill the sheriff's men. Either eventuality should ignite a civil war within la Junta Mixta. But we had to be sure. Sharp suggested we seek out El Jefe and put a burr under his saddle as well. That sounded like a good idea, and we wanted to meet him anyway, but I didn't know how to find the leader of the Mexican bandits.

"How's your Spanish?" Sharp asked.

"Getting better the longer I live in San Diego, but not good. Why?"

"If we get to talk to El Jefe, he'll be surrounded by bandits. They'll likely talk in Spanish in front of us. Pretend ya don't know a word beyond hola, sí, and no."

"Jeff, if they talk fast, I *won't* understand a thing they're saying."

"They'll talk fast all right." He pondered that. "Try anyway. Keep your expression neutral, no matter what you hear."

"Okay." I thought a moment. "Then our immediate problem is getting an audience with El Jefe. Jeff, how would you like to take a ride?"

"Horseback?"

I nodded.

"Hell, yes. Nora keeps me in buggies."

"We'll head south. I heard Mexican highwaymen exact a toll for using El Camino Real. Without someone to set up a meet, it's the fastest way to contact his men. Maybe we can convince them to take us to El Jefe."

"Get robbed? That's your plan?" Sharp laughed and slapped the table. "Great idea, Steve. Let's rent some horses from the hotel. It's a fine day for a ride."

We leaped to our feet and hired a cabriolet back to the hotel. In short order, we checked on the women and Jeffie, talked to my mother, avoided William—still closeted with Jenny—changed clothes, checked our weapons, hired horses, and rode south on the famous El Camino Real, or King's Highway. Soon, we were traveling the route between Misión de San Carlos Borromeo del Rio Carmelo and Misión San Antonio de Padua, a distance of about fifty miles. We had no intention of riding that far, however. The highwaymen were reputed to operate less than five miles outside of Monterey. Before we left, we learned from a stable hand that El Jefe's real name was Carlos Hernández. He had led a local band of banditos for years prior to the formation of la Junta. We were also told that he hates gringos. That attitude seemed to be a common theme for two factions of la Junta Mixta.

Within a short distance, El Camino Real turned inland, and the surroundings were heavily forested, providing a perfect landscape for robbers to jump out unexpectedly. This part of the road was not heavily traveled because the next city was nearly two hundred and fifty miles to the south. The section between San Francisco and Monterey was popular, as was the road between Santa Barbara and San Diego, but only people traversing the entire length of the coast would be on this section of El Camino Real. The scarce traffic proved helpful to highwaymen who preferred to do their work without interference from throngs of travelers with guns.

Sharp and I were armed with rifles and pistols; normal for me, but Sharp seldom carried a pistol. The regally named King's Highway wasn't much more than a wagon-width trail, and in reality, King Alfonso XII had less claim to this road than El Jefe. Virginia, Jeffie, Juanita, and I had traveled up from San Diego in a stagecoach that I had customized as a honeymoon surprise. At the time, we were ignorant about the risk of highwaymen in this area. Aside from the nuisance of stopping to toss coins to miscreants, El Camino Real had been generally safe, especially with an armed teamster and his shotgun-wielding sidekick, both of whom had gone on to San Francisco for more engaging nightlife. I remembered this specific section of highway because this close to Monterey, the wooded beauty had caught our attention. We hadn't been stopped, possibly because we traversed it early in the morning and passed El Jefe's men before they had awakened. I hoped that this time we wouldn't be so lucky.

We had been riding less than two hours when six Mexican bandits pulled in front of us to bar passage. We pulled up and said howdy as friendly as possible.

"Buen día," the lead bandito said, with a tip of his broad-brimmed hat. "You must pay to travel this road, Señor."

"How much?" I asked.

"Two dollars … one each." He shrugged "Everyone must pay."

"We'll pay five dollars each, but only after you take us to El Jefe."

"Five dollars? That is good. We accept your generous offer, but we know no El Jefe."

"Carlos Hernández," I said. "You know him. Otherwise, you couldn't work this section of road."

"No, Señor. I know not of this man either." He smiled. "You pay ten dollars anyways."

"They are the same man … which you already know. Take us to him. He wants to hear what we have to say. Then you get your ten dollars; otherwise …" I let my voice trail off.

"Otherwise?" He laughed. "You told us you have ten dollars. *Estúpido.* Now hand it over, or we take it all."

He smiled again. An engaging smile, which caused me to think I could like this scoundrel under different circumstances.

Then he added, "Otherwise …" letting his voice trail off.

Before the word finished trailing out of his mouth, I had my gun pointed at his chest. Without looking, I knew Sharp had his gun out behind me. The banditos didn't appear concerned.

"Señor, there are six of us. Put the guns away. Your life is worth more than a few dollars."

"Whatever happens in the next few minutes will be no concern of yours," I said. "No matter what else happens, you'll be dead." I tried a smile, albeit considerably less engaging. "But no one needs to die. Just take us to El Jefe. We need to have a little talk with him. If he doesn't like what we have to say, then we can have our gunfight."

"We told you, we know no El Jefe."

"Then I apologize in advance for killing you." I kept my tone pleasant.

"Why do you want to see this ... this boss man?" he asked, seemingly unruffled.

"The sheriff is planning on cheating him. We think he should know."

The bandit shrugged. "The sheriff is a bad man. He cheats all the time. We let him cheat, and he lets us rob *gringos*."

"This scheme will destroy la Junta Mixta," I answered.

That got his attention. He held up a single finger to signal wait and conferred with his compatriots. I could follow the conversations of most Spanish-speaking people in San Diego, but these bandits spoke in rapid whispers. I picked up only a few words, and they were profanities. The bandits were obviously not in agreement. Finally, the argument tapered off, and the leader turned back to me.

"Put your *pistolas* away. We will take you to Don Carlos."

Without another word, he wheeled his horse around and rode into the woods. We holstered our guns and followed.

Chapter 26

I was surprised when the bandits led us to a tidy set of log cabins on a cliff overlooking the Pacific Ocean. The Mexicans I knew in San Diego lived in whitewashed stucco houses. I looked around and saw nothing but trees, so using logs as a primary building material made sense, but from personal experience, I found the dark log structures odd for Mexican dwellings.

We had traveled west at a northerly slant, so I guessed we were less than ten miles south of Monterey. The scenery was breathtaking, the craggy coastline majestic, and the forest pristine and eerily silent. Except for the footfall of wildlife scattering in front of us, we heard nothing due to the thick trees that deadened sound. In fact, the few words spoken between us were in the low voice used prior to Sunday services. Every vista in every direction impressed. El Jefe lived in a stunning environment.

As we approached, I noticed that the log cabins were organized like a small village. I spotted a blacksmith's shop and a general store and heard saloon-like sounds coming from a cabin about double the size of the others. At the precipice of the circle, a whitewashed cabin stood out as the only non-brown structure. A small cross at the top identified the building as a church.

"What do you call this village?" I asked.

"*La nuestra*," the leader responded.

Since I was pretending to not understand any Spanish, I stifled a laugh. *La nuestra* meant "ours." They probably called it something else, but this bandito had a sense of humor.

We rode up to a large cabin and were ordered to dismount. Three of the Mexicans dismounted with us. Sharp and I tied up our horses to a hitching post while the three Mexicans that remained on horseback took the reins of their comrades' horses and rode them down to a corral I could see beyond the saloon. Of course, Mexicans would call the saloon a *cantina*. I had been in many *cantinas* in San Diego and found them brighter and merrier than most saloons.

We were told to wait. Two of the bandits kept an eye on us while the leader entered the cabin. I surveyed the village and saw that all the Mexicans were watching us. Dozens. Some in curiosity, but most with open hostility. I hoped our meeting with El Jefe went well.

After a few minutes, the leader emerged and beckoned us into the cabin. Unlike the hunting lodge exterior, the inside of the cabin was fitted out in the traditional Mexican style: carved wood furniture with painted panels, woven rugs in primary colors, scenic tapestries hanging from the walls, and lively glass vases. It all reminded me of my neighbors' homes in San Diego. Most surprising, the interior walls had been overlaid with wood panels, then stuccoed and whitewashed. The interior was bright and cheery. It also presented the impression of wealth. El Jefe did well for himself, and I bet a good portion of his income came from *La Virgen de Guadalupe.*

The man who had walked up with his hand extended fit the room. He wore black pants with decorative stitching, expensively tooled boots, and an immaculate white shirt with some simple black embroidery. I guessed that the man was in his fifties. He appeared fit except for a paunch that showed signs of too much *cerveza*, or beer as we called it. Unusual for an *hombre Mexicano*, he was clean shaven, his hair cut so short I could see his skull.

"Gentlemen," he said, "welcome to my home. I am Carlos Hernández. May I offer you something to drink?"

Sharp said, "You would make me a happy man if you had Victoria handy."

"Ah, you know Mexican beer. Unfortunately, I have no Victoria, but I can offer you beer from a San Diego brewery. It's made by Carlos Fredenbaen, a friend of mine."

"It's good beer, Jeff. I drink it often." I turned toward our host. "I live in San Diego."

"I know," he said. "You're Steve Dancy. You're staying at the Del Monte. A fine hotel." He gave Sharp an appraising look. "But I don't know your friend."

"May I introduce Jeff Sharp, recently of New Orleans," I answered. "A friend of many years."

He made a hand signal to a woman who then left the room, presumably to fetch drinks. Our host waved us into chairs situated around a fireplace that had been swept clean of ash. In fact, the entire room was spotless. I couldn't see a single blemish on the whitewashed walls, and the rug looked clean enough to eat from.

"While we wait for our beer, tell me why you insisted on seeing me." He smiled. "By the way, you owe my men ten dollars."

I glanced behind me. Two rough-looking hombres stood to either side of the door. Neither were from the party that had stopped us on El Camino Real. I pulled a small leather sack out of my pants pocket and placed it on the table between us.

"There are ten silver dollars in the sack. Since those men don't appear to be around, could you see that they get this?"

"Keep it. They will escort you back to the highway, and you can give it to them then." He crossed his legs in a casual pose. "Now what is the subject of this meeting?"

I nodded behind me. "May we speak freely in front of these men?"

"Sí, of course."

He seemed to have nothing more to add, so I plunged in.

"We had a situation with one of the members of our party. You may know of it, but that man and his situation is not why we're here. We have paid a tariff demanded by his abductors, and he has rejoined our party."

Hernández sat still and expressionless, so I continued.

"We're here about another matter. The sheriff has a separate scheme for a much larger sum of money. He intends to extract it from me, and he does not intend to share this money with la Junta Mixta. If successful, he means to move to San Francisco and live well, with no further connection to la Junta or his office of sheriff. To insure his safety after he leaves Monterey, he will start a war between the tong and his men. He wants to wipe out the tong leadership and eliminate many of their men."

Still no reaction.

"We have spoken to the tong, and they have encouraged us to kill the white men of la Junta." I hesitated, then added. "They may have talked to you about your role in this endeavor."

"We discussed it. The sheriff also came by. Both asked us to stay out of the fight."

"The tong offered you money. I presume the sheriff offered you the entire county to yourself. He's after a very large sum of money, and afterwards he wants the Junta destroyed. He doesn't want to look over his shoulder for the rest of his life."

Hernández shrugged. "That won't be a hardship. If he betrays us, the remainder of his life will be short."

"He's gonna betray ya," Sharp said. "It may go beyond—"

"Ah, here's the beer," Hernández interrupted as he stood. "I hope you like yours chilled. I come from a hot climate and prefer my beer kept on ice."

"Yep, me too," Sharp said as we stood as well. "Colder the better. Don't understand men who like it lukewarm. Tastes like horse piss that way."

"I wouldn't know," Hernández said. "Never tasted horse piss."

Sharp immediately laughed in his hearty manner, and Hernández smiled at the appreciation of his humor.

The beer was served in the thick-glass square goblets often used in San Diego. It was cold, amber hued, and excellent tasting. It certainly was welcome refreshment after riding for several hours.

After we retook our seats, Hernández crossed his legs, sipped his beer, and casually asked, "What do you expect me to do about this, Señor?"

"Staying out of it might work in our interests," I offered.

He seemed genuinely confused. "Perhaps, but then why are you here?"

Sharp laughed. "That's Steve's thinkin'. I propose that ya kill all yer partners." He laughed some more. "Be obliged, of course."

Instead of asking how obliged, Hernández said, "If that is what you want, *amigo*, then you came to the wrong place." He waved his arm around the room, but his words indicated that he meant the whole village. "My duty is to this *pueblo*. To my family, friends, neighbors, and children. My job—El Jefe's job—is to protect them. The tong and the sheriff concern themselves only with their men." He extended both arms out like a sovereign. "I have broader responsibilities."

I understood. Carlos Hernández viewed himself as Don Carlos, and this village as his hacienda. More important, he wanted others to see him that way, not as a bandit chieftain. And why not? He made his living and supported the village by robbing the rich. Robin Hood was part of a long tradition of folk heroes who redistributed wealth at the point of a sword or gun. Since I was one of the rich, my sympathy went only so far, however.

I said, "Jeff was kidding. His sense of humor is not always appropriate. We didn't come here to seek you as an ally, but to assure ourselves that you would remain a noncombatant."

He pondered us for a moment. Finally, he said, "You tell a lie, Señor. If we intended to be a combatant, you would be dead by now. The confirmation of your suspicions would then do you little good. I hear your *madre* has *mucho dinero*. The elimination of your role in this drama would not be missed."

"It would be a poor decision to kill us before we pay the sheriff's extortion."

"Señor, I have no idea what you're talking about. Nor do I care."

Hernández was too smart to manipulate. The direct approach would be better.

I started with, "Señor Hernández, we—"

"What my clumsy friend is tryin' to say," interrupted Sharp, "is that we need yer help. We can't fight the tong *and* the sheriff. We can't even pay them off an' escape assassination afterwards. We're in a pickle. Now … here, in this village, yer Don Carlos, but everywhere else, yer El Jefe, the murderin' bandito. A bad man … not a don. Ya want respectability. We need yer guns. So now yer thinkin', how can they offer respectability in exchange for my support? With lawyers, Mr. Hernández. Not from San Francisco, but the best legal assholes from the great city of New York. A don needs a hacienda. With legal title. San Francisco shysters are breakin' Spanish land grants left an' right, but they get the money from New York to do their dirty work. From people we can get to. Ya mentioned my friend's mother. She's rich as ya say, but also friendly with the right people in New

York. Ya want a hacienda, all legal an' such … we can get it for ya." Sharp paused dramatically. "If we're not dead, that is."

The room remained silent for what seemed like an eternity.

Hernández suddenly stood and extended his hand. When Sharp grasped it, he covered their grip with his other hand.

"Well, in that case, sí, Señores … yes." El Jefe laughed. "Why didn't you explain it like that in the first place?"

Chapter 27

As we traveled back to El Camino Real, Sharp looked extremely pleased with himself. Our escort, made up of the same six bandits, gave us enough space to speak freely. I presumed it was out of respect for our newfound comradery with El Jefe.

"Just so you know, I was about to make the same offer when you butted into the conversation."

"Sure ya were." He gave me a condescending smile. "But I said it better."

I had to laugh. "I suppose you did."

We had agreed to the offer before riding out and had even gotten approval from my mother who would work the New York side of the arrangement. Despite our planning, I was surprised how well it had been received by Hernández. Sometimes luck is more important than a good plan.

Sharp said, "We won us an ally. Now what?"

"I'm open to ideas, but I suggest we wait to see what happens on that fishing boat. If one side kills someone from the other side, we'll have something to work with. That's enough pretext to start a war." I rode a few minutes before adding, "The worst thing that could happen is nothing."

"I don't see nothin' happenin'," Sharp said. "We planted seeds pretty deep. I believe the tong an' sheriff will go at each other ... real serious-like. Knowin' those boys, this plan oughta work. Numbers will be on the tong side. Long-distance weapons on the sheriff's side. By the time Joseph shows up with his Pinkertons, we'll have whittled the numbers down."

Sharp sounded happy. I couldn't share his enthusiasm.

"This was supposed to be a family holiday. A grand holiday at a world-renowned resort. Fun and relaxing. Instead of calm and peaceful, it's been violent and stressful." I hit the horn of my saddle. "And expensive, to boot. This trip is costing a pretty penny."

"Are ya suggestin' yer life ain't worth a penny?"

I laughed. "No, just letting off steam."

"Good. Never let the pressure build so high, somethin' goes pop."

"Like my gun?"

"Yep. Keep yer gun holstered until we got the situation right for us."

I shook my head. "I had the situation right once. Didn't recognize it until later. Had the sheriff one-on-one and didn't shoot him. Could have ended this thing."

"Can't cry over spilt milk," Sharp said.

"Okay, then let's talk about my current problem."

"Shoot," Sharp responded with a chuckle.

I laughed at his choice of word. "All right, here it is. I'm soon going to have a lot of money, and the sheriff knows exactly where I'm at in gathering up his extortion. He wants it deposited in his bank in San Francisco. If I do that, I'll lose all leverage, so I'm bringing it here to Monterey, but I need to handle the money so no one gets their paws on it. My problem is where to put it."

"Ya don't trust the bankers in this town?"

"I used to trust telegraphists. Not anymore. I don't think anyone … or anything has remained untouched by this sheriff. He's corrupted everything."

"Ya trusted the hotel manager with the ransom. That worked out. Why not the extortion money?"

"This is a lot more money. He wouldn't run away and abandon his Del Monte investments for twenty-five thousand. But in all likelihood, he's under the thumb of the sheriff. Reluctantly, but compromised just the same. He's got a daughter, and the sheriff probably keeps him in line by threatening her well-being. I believe he wants to do the right thing, but he'll always choose his daughter over a troublesome guest."

"Steve, if ya don't work with bankers, that means yer holdin' a big pile of cash. Pretty risky."

"Right, that's my problem. Maybe I should transfer the money to a San Francisco bank, but not the sheriff's. At some point, I'll need to prove that I have the funds, but I don't intend to hand over the money unless I have no other way to save my family."

"Ya mean if ya can't shoot yerself clear."

I turned my head to look Sharp in the eye. "Yes. Kill him or pay him. Those are my choices."

We were emerging from a side trail that intersected El Camino Real. When we had a clear view down the road, I saw about ten riders sitting astride horses not a hundred yards to the south. When they spotted us, they immediately wheeled around and galloped right at us. Sharp and I drew our rifles and chambered a round. Was this an ambush? I looked behind me, concerned about what our *nuevos amigos* would do. I grew nervous when they drew their rifles as well, but to my relief, they rode up alongside to face the approaching riders.

The strangers pulled up hard, spraying us with a cloud of dust. They were white, but none wore a deputy's badge. My hope that they might be friendly dissolved with their first words.

"*Gilipollas*, what are you doing with these *americanos?*"

The grimy, unkempt man who had spoken the words looked like an outlaw, and *gilipollas* was a serious insult. Close up, I realized there were only eight of them, so the numbers were equal. That is, if our Mexican escorts were on our side. A big if.

"That's no business of yours," one of the Mexicans said.

"Everything is the Junta's business, amigos. Everything. Have we not made that clear? We've been waiting a long time for your return. Why did you leave your station?"

The grimy man slipped his hand away from his saddle horn and laid it on his pistol handle. I couldn't tell if the menacing gesture and prior *gilipollas* salutation were meaningless bravado or a prelude to deadly gunplay. No one said a word, and I could feel the tension build. In this isolated piece of forest, the only sound I heard was the squeak of shifting butts on leather saddles.

"Answer my questions … or there will be trouble," the grimy man said.

"We took these men to El Jefe because—"

"Do you know these Mexicans?" I demanded of the grimy man. "The sheriff said we were to be left alone, but these highwaymen tried to rob us, and when we didn't hand over our money, they abducted us. At least El Jefe understood that we're not to be bothered, so he ordered these men to return us to the road."

"Shut up!" the leader yelled. "I'm not talking to you. Now, *gilipollas,* answer me. Truthfully … or I'll kill you right here and now."

A couple of the horses bucked slightly, and the situation became even tenser. I was trying to figure out what I could say to lighten the mood, when Sharp spoke up.

"Hey, dumb shit, ya want trouble? I can accommodate ya."

Everyone froze at the words. Our side had drawn rifles, cocked, but pointed skyward. Only one man on the other side had the forethought to unsheathe his rifle. The rest of them sat on their horses unready, with only a few gripping their pistol handles. The sheriff's men arrogantly believed that no one would ever challenge them. They were taken aback by Sharp's words.

I made a quick calculation. We could win this fight. The numbers were even, and we had a readiness advantage. Perhaps it was time to get into this war for real. Right here. Right now.

"Who the hell are you?" the grimy man asked.

"A man with a rifle who knows how to use it," Sharp answered.

The grimy man pointed at the two of us. "Git. This is a family argument. Go back to your swank hotel and stay the hell out of our way."

I said, "If you're looking for money, we don't have any. I already gave it to that man riding next to you."

"What?" The grimy man turned to his sidekick. "What's he—?"

Without a signal, we all knew that this was the moment to shoot. I dropped my rifle barrel and shot the sidekick center chest. I heard a cascade of shots. Loud, booming noises. Some close to my ears. I shifted to the next outlaw, but he twisted in such an unnatural way that it told me someone else had shot him. I moved my aim further left, but my bullet was only one of many that knocked that rider clean out of the saddle. I could hardly see through the gun smoke as I searched for another target. I spotted an outlaw in the rear trying to wheel his horse around to run, but I shot him before he could complete the turn.

I scanned the opposition. Only one man remained astride his horse. The grimy man. His look of utter bewilderment was comical. I laughed. Each man had assumed that everyone else would go after the leader, so each of us had picked another target. The grimy man remained unscathed. He had drawn his pistol, but it was pointed at a downward slant. The fight had happened so fast, he hadn't even gotten his gun up to sight on a target. He remained as still as a bronze statue in a city park.

Now what? We couldn't have him warning the sheriff that we had joined with El Jefe. A forewarned sheriff would endanger us all, including my family.

I shot him. As I did, he was simultaneously hit by at least five bullets, probably more. The grimy man fired once, but the bullet went harmlessly into the ground in front of us. He flipped over backwards and plopped into the dirt with a cloud of dust. He never even shuddered after he landed.

I instantly turned in my saddle to survey our side of the fight. Everyone remained on his horse, but two of the Mexicans had wounds seeping blood. I walked my horse over to the closest and saw a graze across his cheek. It would leave a scar he could brag about. The other man appeared to be hurt worse. He started to fall, but two of his companions jumped off their horses and helped him slide to the ground.

I dismounted to check the sheriff's men to make sure they wouldn't cause more trouble. Only one of the white outlaws seemed as if he might recover from his wounds. As I was about to kneel to examine him, I heard a shot at my shoulder, and a bullet hit him between the eyes. When I swiveled to look behind me, I saw one of the Mexicans with his rifle snug against his shoulder, aiming down at the unfortunate outlaw.

"These *yanquis* treat us like *mierda*." He spit on him. "Now he messes his pants. The world is better without him."

He stomped away.

I looked over at Sharp, who remained mounted and seemed relaxed. I walked over.

"Bloody mess," I said.

"Yup. Caught 'em unawares. Damn massacres make me feel soiled." Just when I thought he might get maudlin, Sharp grinned. "Sure happy we made it out whole, though."

Chapter 28

The Mexicans gave us the same instructions as the outlaws. They told us to go back to our hotel and stay put until we heard from El Jefe. They would get rid of the bodies and cover the blood on the highway. They also informed us that the horses, saddlery, and other possessions were theirs, but they appreciated our help in killing the sheriff's men. Generous of them.

We rode off.

After a while, Sharp said, "Say somethin'."

"What?"

"Say that again."

"What?" I said louder, with a bit of frustration.

"I hear like I'm in a deep well … but … I *can* hear." He shook his head like he had something in his ears. "Damn Mexican fired his rifle inches from my ear." He paused before adding, "Hell, probably a couple feet, but it sounded damn close."

"You think we did the right thing?" I asked.

"Steve, we want civil war. That'll get it started all right … along with some poor coolie dyin' out at sea on a fishin' boat."

"I'm not so sure that fishing boat coolie has anything to fear," I mused out loud.

"What do ya mean?"

"Forewarned is forearmed. The tong will be ready, and they'll kill the sheriff's men instead of the other way around. I'm getting the impression that the sheriff didn't run a fair-minded gang. Hernández was too easy to win over, and the tong have shown no loyalty to the Junta." I walked my horse a few paces before adding, "The Junta may have been a name that represented only a temporary truce rather than a real outlaw coalition. I suspect the sheriff will suffer more losses today than those we killed here."

"How many men does he have?" Sharp asked.

"I heard six deputies, but I've only seen Sam and Rod. I don't know how many without a badge, but eight less now. From a skill perspective, the deputies are a cut above those ruffians we just encountered."

"Encountered?" Sharp laughed. "That's a pleasant way of puttin' it."

When we arrived at the hotel, we rode directly to the stables to return the horses and gear.

As we dismounted, the stable hand asked, "You men been down by the docks?"

"Naw," Sharp said agreeably. "We took a ride along yer beautiful coastline. Grand view of the ocean."

"Then you missed all the action," the stable hand said excitedly.

"Action?" I asked, amused because we had seen plenty of action. "Down at the docks? What happened?"

"Them Chinese got rowdy, and the sheriff went down to calm things. Killed a bunch in an awful fight. Two deputies killed too, and another got a nasty gash along his arm."

"How many Chinese?" I asked.

"Hell, I don't know." He started speaking fast and waving his arms for emphasis. "The sheriff and his men blew the hell out of them ... with shotguns and rifles and pistols. The tong fought with knives mostly. Got their ass kicked. Lots of chinks dead. And I heard that rivers of blood flowed into the ocean, turning the sea redder than a brandy-new bandanna. The chinks dragged away their dead and wounded, so no one knows how many really got killed, but there was lots. Everybody says so. Townsfolk are up in arms because there's plenty more of them Chinese, spread all over, and they like to slit your throat while you sleep. Some of the businessmen want the sheriff to quarantine them wharf side. Our coolies, the Del Monte's, didn't show up for work after the shift change, so maybe it's already happening."

"Were ya there?" Sharp asked.

He appeared to take umbrage at the question. "Well, no, I had to work, but I heard all about it from someone in the kitchen. Two people in the kitchen, in fact. Both were there, and they told me straight."

"Did they now?" Sharp asked pointedly.

"Come on, mister. I heard it firsthand." He looked chagrined. "The story's all over town. Just like I said it."

I gave the hand a half-dollar, and Sharp and I left the stable. Neither of us spoke until we were well out of earshot.

"What do ya think?" Sharp asked.

"I think we better get the straight story before we jump to conclusions."

"The sheriff ain't a shy man. If he suspected the tong was conspirin' against him, he might just go down to the docks an' kill a bunch of 'em. Strong message … delivered hard an' fast. That's his style."

"Could be, or maybe something else provoked an uprising. We need to find out what really happened."

"How?"

"We'll start with the manager," I answered. "He seems to know everything that's happening in this town."

As we entered the lobby, a highly agitated bellman ran over. "Mr. Dancy, Mr. Sharp, thank goodness you've returned. Your womenfolk are desperate to talk to you. They want you upstairs right away. Now!"

Without responding, I automatically gave the boy a quarter and bounded up the stairs to the second floor. As soon as I hit our landing, I froze. Four rough-looking men guarded the hallway. Sharp and I carried our rifles in sheaths, intent on returning them to our rooms. I considered releasing the leather tie, but my Colt was a better weapon in close quarters anyway. I shifted my rifle to my left hand and walked forward.

"Why are you men in our hallway?" I asked one of them, none too friendly.

"Waiting for you." He squared off against me. "Sheriff's orders. You're to come with us."

"Show me your badge," I ordered.

"Ain't got badges. There's been a battle down at the docks, and the sheriff deputized us in a hurry."

"Then get your ass back down to his office and get badges."

The man appeared briefly confused but then barked, "You're coming with us."

"I'm not. In fact, don't you leave just yet. I want to check on my family and make sure they're unharmed."

"Unharmed?" He chuckled. "Yup, I guess you could say they was unharmed in the way you mean … but they won't be if you don't come along quiet-like."

I almost killed him right then and there but took a long breath before asking, "Are some of your men inside my rooms?"

"Don't need 'em." He puffed up. "We can take care of this little errand."

"No, you can't," I said flatly. "Send one of your men to knock on my door and have my wife stick her head out. I want to talk to her."

He took a belligerent step toward me. "Talk to her after you return from the sheriff's office."

Sharp stood behind and to the side of me, giving him a clear shot at two of the men. That meant the ones on the other side of the hall were mine. I tried to subdue my rage. It was best to remain emotionless in a fight. Fear or anger gave the other party an advantage. I should know. I had incited both emotions to get the upper hand in gunfights. Whatever was on the other side of that door was there. I couldn't change it. But I wasn't leaving with these men, which meant I needed to keep my anger in check, especially if this escalated into a gunfight.

Without turning, I said, "Jeff, your rifle unsheathed?"

"Don't worry about it. Let's just kill these men. Ya got the two on the right."

The man suddenly threw up his arms. "No, wait. No need for gunplay. Hell, it's just an errand. You men hold steady, and we'll go get this straightened out with the sheriff. Bring back badges too."

"Stay put. You're not leaving until I see my wife. Bring her to the door."

"Hell, she's fine. I was just trying to rattle you. You know how it is."

"No, I don't know how it is. That's why I want to see her."

"Which one's your wife?" he asked tentatively.

"The older one," I answered automatically, thinking only of Virginia and Jenny.

He laughed. "That old hag. I thought she might be your mother. Hell, she's right as rain."

I flipped my rifle up, grabbed the end of the barrel, and rammed the butt as hard as I could into the man's face. I hit him square on the bridge of his nose, and I heard the cartilage crushed into his skull. I pulled back to hit him again, when I noticed the other men were going for their guns. Damn it. I dropped the rifle and went for my pistol, hitting the wall with my shoulder to get behind the collapsing man I had just hit. The first shot rang out from the next man on my side of the hall. I grabbed the lapels of the man I had bludgeoned and tried to pull him in front of me. I saw other muzzle flashes, one from my side of the hall and two from the men on Sharp's side. I jerked my human shield away from the wall and extended my arm behind his head, firing at the second man on my side. I shot him three times before I shifted my attention to the other men. Both remained standing but writhed in pain. I shot them both again.

If the outdoor shooting had been noisy and hazy, the confines of the hallway made this fight ten times worse. If Virginia opened the door to see what was happening, I would never see her through the gun smoke. My ears rang, my eyes stung, and my throat felt raspy. The battle seemed like it had lasted for at least ten minutes, but I knew that was an illusion. The fight had lasted under five seconds.

I glanced behind me and felt relief to see Sharp still standing. I surveyed our assailants. None were dead yet, but three of them would die soon. I still held up the man I had clubbed. His bloody face appeared lifeless. Then I felt my shirtfront getting wet. Had I been shot? I let go of the body, and it fell to the floor. My entire front was soaked in blood. I ran my hand over my stomach and felt a wound. I probed a hole in my shirt with my finger and could feel a bullet just inside my skin. That didn't make sense. Then I reexamined the man on the floor. He had been shot at least twice. I kicked him over with my foot. One exit wound. Damn. The bullet had spent its energy passing through his body, or at least most of its energy. I began to feel pain in my stomach.

Someone put his hand on my shoulder and turned me around. Out of fear or shock, I almost fired my Colt but recognized Sharp at the last moment. I wasn't reacting right. What was happening? My stomach hurt like hell, and Sharp's mouth was moving, but I couldn't hear what he was saying. I felt wobbly. Is this what it was like to get shot? I didn't know. I didn't know because I always won my gunfights.

My legs felt weak, and I knew Sharp was holding me up. I was passing out.

The last thing I saw was Virginia's face hovering over me.

She had a swollen face that nearly closed one eye.

Chapter 29

I opened my eyes to see an unkempt beard and bloodshot eyes. Right in my face. I blinked. I blinked again. What happened? How did I get here? For that matter, where was I? I closed my eyes again and tried to think straight, but my thoughts wouldn't go in a straight line long enough to figure anything out. I opened my eyes again to the bloodshot eyes, scraggly beard, and stinky breath.

I remembered. Hell, I had been shot. Virginia was in danger. She had been hurt. Where was she? Where was my son? I tried to lift myself but barely budged. I tried to speak, but only low mumbles came out. Still, I seemed to have gotten the attention of the bearded one. He pulled away from my face and looked down at me as if pondering a lost child, one he had no idea what to do with.

"How do you feel?" he asked, not unkindly.

How do I feel? Nothing. I felt nothing. I swallowed. My mouth was as dry as a used dishrag left hanging overnight. It tasted just as nasty. The bearded man lifted my head and gave me a sip of water. Then another. Water had never tasted so good.

After he gently returned my head to the pillow, I answered, "Not bad. No pain, but my stomach feels ... pinched." I moved my head from side to side, but I didn't recognize the room. "Where's my wife? My son?"

"The next room. All your party is in the next room. Your wife was getting in my way, so I sent her out." He smiled slightly. "You're a lucky man. That bullet was spent by the time it hit you. It didn't penetrate the muscle. Skin deep, as they say. I pulled it out with no problem and gave you three stitches … and a bit of laudanum. That groggy feeling will go away soon. You can stand when you feel able."

I swung my legs around and tried to sit. Too fast. Pain in the gut. I fell back against the table.

"I said stand. Sitting bends the abdomen. You'll probably take your meals standing for the next couple of days."

He checked my stitches.

After he nodded approval, I said, "Help me to my feet."

He instructed me to remain on my back while he swiveled me around until my feet dangled. Then he got to my side, held my arm and shoulder, and helped me stand without bending. Once on my feet, I sighed in relief. The pain was no worse than on my back. I took one tentative step and then another. After a few steps, the dizziness seemed to subside a bit. Once I gained some confidence, I slowly paced the room, and all the while, the bearded man clucked approval.

"Very good," he said. "Much better than I expected. You'll do even better as the laudanum wears off.

"Where's my friend Jeff Sharp?" I asked, trying unsuccessfully to increase my pace.

"Protecting the women. He told me to fix you up proper and get you up and about." His expression turned sympathetic. "I'm afraid he doesn't think this is over."

"Nor do I." Four more shuffle steps, then I added, "Thank you. I assume you're a doctor."

"Veterinarian. I work for the Del Monte and take care of the hotel's livestock." He shrugged. "I was handy … and I know how to keep quiet."

I looked around again. The room had no windows, but the whitewash and gas lanterns kept it from being overly dark.

"Where are we?"

"Basement of a hotel out building. The manager hid you and your party down here until I could get you well enough to travel. I'm afraid your presence has become too burdensome. Your mother has already made some kind of arrangements, I believe."

"Mr. Nelson wants us gone?"

He appeared astonished by my question. "You're surprised. He's a good man, but you can't blame him. You killed four men in his hotel, endangering other guests, not to mention the fisticuffs in the dining room. There's been a bloody battle down by the docks and rumors of another gunfight out of town on El Camino Real. There's a damn war going on, and you brought it inside his hotel. He needs to protect his business and family."

I kept walking and tried to clear my head. "I can't think straight. Why'd you give me laudanum for three damn stitches?"

"I don't work on humans that often, except to pull teeth. I found laudanum makes it easier for the patient."

"I think you mean easier for you," I said, a bit more harshly than intended.

"That too." He hesitated. "Your friend was also angry about the laudanum. Said you might need to go back into battle."

"He was right." I wanted to say more, but I didn't have enough energy to argue. Instead, I leaned against the wall and said, "I want to see my wife." When he didn't move, I added in a soft voice, "Now please."

He nodded and stuck his head outside the room and spoke quietly. In short order, Virginia came rushing in.

"Steve, are you okay?"

"That's my question for you. What happened before we got back?"

She touched her eye. "You mean this? It's nothing. Don't worry about it. Jenny and I got into a tussle with those men. I tried to hit one with a lamp, but he blocked it and slugged me." She put a restraining hand on my chest. "Relax, they didn't do any more … but … they threatened to after they took care of you and Jeff. They bragged that they would kill Jeff, hog-tie you and William, and rape us with you both in the room. That's when Jenny went berserk, so I tried to hit one of them with the lamp." She looked down at my stomach. "I know you were shot, but Jenny's actually in worse shape. They beat her mercilessly. I was lucky to have been knocked out with a single punch. They left me alone after that. From what I hear, she fought like a tigress."

I nodded. When Jenny was fifteen, she had been raped by two men who forced her husband to watch. It didn't surprise me that she would never allow that to happen again.

"What about William? Did he help her fight?"

Virginia's jaw set. "No … he blustered at first, but one punch to the gut and he folded."

"Jeffie, Mother, Nora, Juanita?" I asked.

"Everyone's fine. They didn't touch anyone else. They might have if they had won that fight in the hallway, but thank goodness you and Jeff arrived ready to act."

I wasn't going to tell her about our earlier gunfight, not now at least. It occurred to me that the fight on the El Camino Real had put us in an alert frame of mind for when we ascended the stairs. The outcome may have been different if we had been more relaxed and caught unawares.

"I'm sorry, I feel groggier than if I was drunk. You said Jenny was hurt bad? How bad?"

"Broken jaw, cracked ribs, black eyes, big hunk of hair pulled out. They really went after her. Steve, they—"

I interrupted her. "Does Jenny have a doctor or this veterinarian?"

"The vet treated her. First. He laid you on the table and gave you laudanum to keep you comfortable until he could get to you. Sharp almost punched him when he found out."

I heard Sharp's voice. "I would have too, 'cept we needed him to fix your sorry ass."

I hadn't heard Sharp come into the room. He was a welcome sight, but the steaming coffee in his hand was more welcome. He handed it to me, and I took a cautious sip. Coffee had never tasted better.

Why were doctors so eager to administer laudanum? We had had the same argument with a doctor in Silverton who over-sedated McAllen after a far more severe gunshot wound. Quiet patients make their life easier, I guess. At least I had been given only one dose. I considered my condition, and after a moment, concluded that I had no craving for the drug.

"How's yer head?" Sharp asked.

"Like someone's been rearranging it with a ball-peen hammer. But I'm better than I was five minutes ago." I pushed away from the wall and took a few more tentative steps. "As least I can move around on my feet."

"Yer a lucky cuss," Sharp chortled. "Not many get gut shot an' live to tell the tale."

I gently rubbed my stomach and felt a heavy bandage under my shirt. "I don't feel lucky. In fact, this makes me wonder if my luck's running out. I've never been so much as nicked in a gunfight before."

Sharp suddenly became serious. "Ya want me to tell ya what ya did wrong?"

"No need. I let my emotions get the better of me. I felt such rage; I slammed my rifle butt into that son of a bitch's face. Then when I needed my Colt, both hands were full of a rifle pointed the wrong direction."

Sharp nodded. "Glad ya know. Don't do that again."

"I'll try to remember, but if I believe they've hurt my family again, I don't know if I can stay calm. I tried to ram that rifle butt all the way through his skull. I wanted him dead in the worst way."

Sharp nodded. "I understand. Just remind yerself that the objective is to win the fight. If ya lose, yer useless to yer family … an' me."

"Understood," I said.

This was a harsh reproach from Sharp. We had been in several fights together and trusted each other. More than trust, we knew what the other would do at any given moment. I had let him down, and it had been almost catastrophic for both of us. I vowed to keep my head next time. And there would be a next time. We had started this war, and now we were in the midst of it.

"How's Jenny taking it?"

"She's got to be hurting, but she acts like she doesn't care," Virginia said. "She's been glum for a couple of days, so when those men came in, she acted like she couldn't care less until they threatened rape; then she became crazed with rage. When I came around, she was a bloody mess and mentally detached. She showed emotion only after she learned the men were dead. Then she pounded the table in joy, because she couldn't speak."

We had caused this. We shouldn't have started the fight before McAllen arrived. Damn it. I shoved the thought away. I couldn't focus on how our little war had endangered my family. I needed to get my thinking straight so I could help in the coming fight.

I asked, "Jeff, have you learned anything about the fight at the docks?"

"A bit. Laundry room gossip says the sheriff went down there, guns blazin' for no apparent reason. Supposedly, dozens killed, includin' two deputies. Normal Chinese are frightened as hell. No one seems to understand what's happenin'."

"Tong leadership?"

"Intact, as far as I know." Sharp shook his head and appeared truly sad. "In battle, soldiers die before generals."

"How about our fight on El Camino Real?"

"Whispers by locals, but officially, nothin' happened. Sheriff was at the newspaper office, so I 'xpect the public will be told a pack of lies 'bout both skirmishes."

"So we got us a war, but so far, it's a secret war."

"Only the dyin' know."

"Well, a few only gut shot know as well."

Sharp chuckled. "True enough, but some might say ya deserved it for startin' this little donnybrook."

"Some might say."

I leaned my buttocks against the operating table, being careful to keep my stomach straight. "But now that the plan has worked, what'll we do next?"

"The plain truth?" Sharp asked.

That got my attention. "Give it to me straight."

"We wanted to use the tong and the Mexicans to whittle down the whites. That idea worked somewhat on that road, but it looks like the sheriff outsmarted us at the docks. Instead of goin' after a couple of fishin' boat coolies, he made a surprise attack on the tong. From what I hear, he overwhelmed their warrior class before they knew what hit 'em. The tong fights best in close quarters, but the sheriff shot 'em up beyond the reach of their knives and fists. However, the deputies who died were shot. The tong ain't against usin' firearms; it just ain't their favorite way to fight."

"The sheriff's forces must be depleted some," I mused. "We killed eight on the road, and two of his deputies are dead."

"I 'xpect those on the road were dumb-ass outlaws. Whether true or not, I heard they weren't real members of la Junta. The sheriff took a large posse to the docks, so he probably sent minions out to check on the Mexicans. I haven't learned if the two killed at the docks were official deputies or ruffians sworn in for the shootin' party."

"Damn, got any good news?"

"Yer alive." He smiled. "Yer family and friends are safe."

"William?"

"He's okay, but worthless in a fight. Don't make plans that count on him."

"How long do we have?" I wondered out loud. "The Del Monte manager wants us out as soon as I'm able to move."

Sharp grinned. "You're lookin' sickly. Better lie down an' get some rest until I get back."

I started to laugh but winced in pain. I asked, "Where are you going?"

"Yer mother decided we needed to get away from here. Fast. She sent our luggage ahead to the train station an' bought tickets for all of us to San Francisco. The train leaves in less than three hours. Not enough time for her private car to be brought around, so she'll meet up with it again in San Francisco. We decided to use a hotel carriage to get to the station 'cuz your stagecoach would be a telltale sign we were runnin'. She composed a letter for the sheriff tellin' him his fracas at the docks made us feel unsafe remainin' in Monterey. She wrote that you'll travel back with two satchels of cash as soon as it's ready. The sheriff won't buy it, so I want to check out the route an' station."

"My mother miscalculated," I protested. "The sheriff will never let us leave town."

"She knows that. The letter's meant to be read after we're gone. She wants to sow a little confusion in his mind. Make him wonder if yer still gonna pay. Otherwise, he'll kill ya outright. Hopefully, he ain't got wind of our departure, but I want to check the route to the train station just in case he has."

"Jeff, you can't go by yourself." I pushed my buttocks away from the table and winced again. "I'll go with you."

"Hell, no. In case ya haven't noticed, I changed outta my gentleman clothes. Not many have seen me in these duds. People pay no nevermind to an old coot in threadbare clothes."

Sharp was dressed in clean but worn work clothes. He didn't look like a wealthy gentleman or even a rancher—more like a carpenter dressed in his after work outfit. I had to admit, he looked entirely different. Most people wouldn't give him a second look. To accent his point, he threw on a sweat-stained cowboy hat and pulled it down over his eyes.

"Jeff, be careful," Virginia said.

"Ain't I always?"

Chapter 30

An hour later, the house veterinarian pronounced me fit to leave his care. I could not dissuade him from his diagnosis, nor would he delay telling Nelson. His instructions to me were clear: change the dressing daily and do not lift anything heavy. I quit arguing. My head felt clear, and the pain was tolerable. Virginia led me by the arm into the next room.

Juanita was playing with Jeffie to distract him from the tension, but when he spotted me, he broke away from her and rushed my legs. Virginia picked him up so I wouldn't need to bend over to greet our son. After some hugs and kisses, Juanita took him back to the corner to toss around a rubber ball.

William sat away from the women, looking forlorn. He kept rubbing his stomach as if it still hurt, which was unlikely. I ignored him.

The problem was Jenny.

She was conscious but looked horrid. Her face was swollen, eyes black, the side of her face bruised severely. She lay on a table, glaring at the ceiling, making no attempt to move or speak. Nora tried to dab her face with a wet towel, but Jenny remained indifferent. Mother watched them both with a look full of purpose. I knew that look. It meant she was plotting revenge.

The veterinarian said that Jenny should suffer no permanent damage, but I wondered how he could know. She appeared badly hurt.

"What about her jaw?" I asked.

"A fracture only. There's no treatment. In a couple of days, the swelling will recede and the bruising fade. Her jaw will realign, and she'll begin to feel normal. Talking will be painful for a while, but her jaw will soon function without pain. For travel, the more serious problem is her ribs. They will make movement painful."

"Including the jostling of a railcar?" my mother asked.

"Yes."

Jenny crooked a finger and jabbed it at the door.

Virginia asked, "You want to go?"

Jenny nodded. I had no doubts about Jenny handling the pain of travel.

The veterinarian said, "Then I will leave you to plan your departure."

He climbed the stairs to the upper level, not wanting to hear how or when we were leaving. That suited me just fine. I didn't know or trust the man.

William got up and appeared as if he were leaving as well.

"Where are you going, young man?" my mother demanded.

"I'm not part of this, and no one cares about me. I'm going to stay in the hotel until the dust clears."

"You will not," my mother said in a tone I had heard plenty of times as a child that continued to scare me to this day. "Sit down here. You have an obligation to protect your wife. Be a man, for Christ's sake. You've lived a soft, easy life, and now it's time to pay the piper. You will do your part and quit your incessant whining. Understood?"

Without replying, William went back to his corner and sat down.

I walked over to a hat tree to retrieve my Colt. After cinching my holster belt, I picked up my rifle, which leaned against the wall. I needed to find Jeff Sharp before I could allow the women out of this cellar.

"Where do you think you're going?" Virginia asked.

"Jeff went to see if the route to the station is clear. He hasn't returned. Everyone stay put until I get back."

"He went by himself?" Mother asked.

"He did."

Virginia moved between me and the stairs. "And you're going to traipse after him by yourself? With your belly sewn up like a Thanksgiving turkey?" She wheeled on my mother. "Did you raise your son to be foolish?"

"I did not," she said flatly. "We're going with you. Virginia, carry your pistol and that heavy purse of yours. I'll carry a rifle. Any questions?" Without waiting for a reply, she added, "Good. Let's go."

I might have argued with Virginia, or even my mother, but it was futile to take them both on at once. I hefted my rifle, prepared to climb to the first floor. To my relief, Sharp came bounding down the stairs.

"Clear," Sharp said, out of breath. "In fact, I think we should git soon. I have a closed carriage outside. The sooner we're at the station, the sooner we'll be surrounded by other people."

"Are you sure it's safe?" my mother asked.

"As safe as it's ever gonna get."

He smiled broadly before adding, "I've got good news."

"The sheriff is dead!" Mother exclaimed.

"No," Sharp responded with a laugh. "But almost as good. Joseph McAllen has arrived ... with a team of Pinkertons."

"Where? Where is he?" I asked, feeling unbelievable relief.

"Scoutin' the path to the rail station. He's figurin' out how to get us there unharmed."

This was excellent news. I could hardly disguise my relief. The women jumped and hugged and jabbered away at each other. I even saw tears in Virginia's eyes. We had all been under far more stress than I had realized. Only William looked befuddled rather than excited.

I grabbed Sharp's elbow to lead him to a corner.

"Where do you think you're going?" my mother demanded.

"Just away from your jubilation to do a little planning," I answered.

"No, Son, you'll do it right here, where we can all hear. No secrets. This affects all of our lives."

I nodded agreement and took a deep breath before addressing everyone in the room. "Please excuse me if I ramble, but my head's still somewhat addled by the laudanum. I wanted to talk to Jeff about how to get to the station safely. Here's my concern. I'm worried that the sheriff will discover our attempt to escape. We have three men, five women, one child ... and a single carriage. That'll be a tight fit. The limited space means it'll be difficult to shoot from inside the carriage, and the wood panels won't stop a bullet coming at us. In my opinion, we shouldn't try to be sneaky. My suggestion is that Jeff and I ride alongside ... horseback. The women and Will should hold rifles out the window so they can be seen from outside. With Joseph and his team in town, I think we should go with a show of strength."

"That sacrifices concealment and surprise!" Virginia exclaimed. "People are watching the hotel. The sheriff will know!"

"He will." I turned to Sharp. "Jeff, with Joseph's protection, what do you think … sneak or show of force?"

He rubbed his chin. "The sheriff ain't no dummy. He's gotta have watchers … an' probably people workin' at this hotel on his payroll. I doubt we'll get outta here unnoticed, so … I think we ride to either side of the carriage." Then he looked at the women and grinned. "If we're alongside, you ladies will avoid shootin' us, right?"

"No promises," my mother responded. "Get in the way of a clear shot at that sheriff, and I just might use a round to knock you off your horse."

"In that case, I'll ride on the opposite side," Sharp chuckled. "If ya got a mind to, ya can have at yer son."

The excessive gaiety was less a measure of humor than relief that we finally had help. I was sure my mother wasn't serious. At least, pretty sure.

"Steve, you're not in shape to ride," Virginia interjected when the merriment settled down.

"I'm fine. Stitches are nothing. The laudanum is what impaired me, not a tiny cut. I'll be more useful riding alongside … and more comfortable." I turned to Sharp. "Jeff, do you need to get horses?"

"Yep. Ya watch these womenfolk, an' I'll be back in three shakes of a lamb's tail."

As he disappeared up the staircase, I realized that Sharp's light banter reflected not only relief for himself, but also his excitement about a possible reprieve for Nora.

From behind me, Virginia asked, "Steve, are you sure?"

Turning away from the staircase, I said, "Absolutely. I can ride just fine, and with McAllen in the mix, I feel confident. We'll get to the train station, no problem."

"I hope those aren't famous last words," my mother said testily.

Chapter 31

Sharp's return wasn't nearly as quick as promised, and time was short to get to the train before departure. When Sharp opened the cellar door and yelled to get moving, everyone, including Jenny, moved at once. No one wanted to dally.

The veterinarian came back down to assist Jenny, who shrugged off his helping hand. Just before my mother climbed the stairs, she gave the veterinarian a few bills and kissed him on the cheek. I believe he was more pleased with the money.

As we climbed, I asked her, "What about our things? Do we need to—"

"Everything important is already at the train station," my mother said irritably. "Did you think I napped while you were taking a laudanum holiday?"

I laughed, but she gave me a harsh look. Her expression said it was not a time for levity. Despite her annoyance, it was amusing that she thought paying someone to pack and transport our things was an accomplishment. I didn't comment further, however. My mother was easier to handle when people complied with her wishes.

"The letter?" Sharp asked when we emerged from the building.

My mother answered. "It will be delivered to the sheriff an hour after the train leaves."

The women clambered aboard the coach while Sharp and I stood guard. We had exited the outbuilding on the side opposite the hotel, and I saw no threats from the low-lying vegetable gardens that spanned a couple of acres to the east. Virginia and my mother sat at the curtained window with rifles at the ready. Juanita sat upright in the center with Jeffie on her lap. Jenny sat on the opposite bench in the center, her back to the driver. Nora guarded the opposite window with a small caliber pistol, and William sat across from her with a scattergun. I knew Jenny was a better shot than either of them and possessed a firmer hand in a fight, but her swollen eyes and other injuries made her next to useless. When I looked inside to make sure everyone was settled, I instructed my mother to switch places with William. I didn't want our two weakest fighters on the same side. After everyone was in place, I wondered how Jeff and I would have fit. My regular teamster and his partner remained in San Francisco, and looking at our hired driver, I noticed that there was room for someone to ride shotgun.

I took Sharp to the side and asked, "Can Nora shoot?"

"Yep … can't hit nothin' though." He looked back at the carriage. "What ya thinkin'?"

"Maybe someone should ride shotgun."

Sharp looked at the driver's seat and then at the passenger compartment. "Let's put a Pink up there. Someone who knows how to wield a shotgun. 'Sides, the driver's nervous enough. He'll feel better with a professional beside him."

"Did you tell him what this is about?"

"Of course. Otherwise he might bolt at the first sign of trouble."

"How much?" I asked.

"One hundred for each passenger delivered safe to the train depot."

I whistled but patted Sharp on the shoulder to let him know I approved.

Now the priority was to find McAllen and his team of Pinkertons. Knowing the captain, that would not be difficult. He would find us.

I came around the rented horse, and Sharp tossed me the reins. I swung into the saddle with a sigh of relief. I felt little pain, and glancing down, I saw no blood seeping into my shirt from beneath the bandage.

Sharp yelled at the teamster to drive. With a snap of the whip, the coach lurched forward, and we rounded the outbuilding to the drive that led away from the hotel. As we came around the hotel, the Great Lawn sloping toward the sea reminded me of our picnic on our first day, when William and I had tossed a football around until I begged off to play with Jeffie. I could feel my anger rising. How dare that ignoble sheriff threaten my family? He'd ruined an otherwise grand holiday. When we reached the gravel path that led to the street, Sharp yelled at the driver to pull up.

Oh, damn. The sheriff and a half dozen of his men sat on horseback, looking up at us. They blocked our exit from the hotel grounds. I looked beyond the sheriff and his men but saw no hint of McAllen or his men. Surely, he had surveyed the road to the train station by now. I nudged my horse forward until I came in sight of Sharp on the other side of the coach.

"Jeff, what do you think?" I yelled across the horses. "Ride up to them or wait for McAllen to show?"

"If we linger, we miss the train." He looked all around us and saw nothing. Still, he added, "Joseph won't fail us. He's around."

I looked at the surroundings ahead. I saw little to obstruct the view to the sea. Few buildings. Few trees. No swale. No place to hide. Would strategic retreat be our best option?

"What is it?" William yelled. "Why are we stopped?"

Sharp spit, then said, "Sheriff's got a welcome party for us at the entrance to the grounds."

"Go back," William yelled.

"That's what he wants," I answered. "If we don't go now, we miss the train."

"Well then, get on with it, Son," my mother yelled. "I want to make that train, and those seven men won't stop me."

Sharp said to the driver, "You heard the lady. Move this carriage down the road, slow and careful-like."

The driver looked anxious but gently snapped the reins.

As we proceeded toward the main road, something odd happened. The sheriff and his men retreated. The sheriff simply smiled, wheeled his horse around, and trotted off with his men in tow. What was that soulless miscreant up to?

I pulled the reins and let the wagon pass so I could ride up to Sharp on the other side.

"What do you think that was about?" I asked Sharp.

Sharp stood in his stirrups and examined the road ahead. "Not sure," he answered. "Maybe he wants a more private spot to confront us. Whatever the reason, he sure as hell ain't gonna let us get away scot-free. I 'xpect he'll waylay us further down the road."

Sharp had scouted the trail, so I asked, "Where would you set up an ambush?"

"It's about three miles to the train station, but there's a crook in the road in about a mile or so. Not many people, an' ya can't see around the bend. That's where I'd do it."

I rode silent, thinking, then asked, "Any ideas?"

"None," he answered.

"How sharp of a bend?"

"Sharp enough we won't be able to get a runnin' start. Not with that coach. Plus, if I were them, I'd put a tree 'cross the road. Make the turn at high speed, an' we just plow right into it."

Damn, we couldn't just walk into their trap. If they challenged us from behind cover, we wouldn't stand a chance. Especially if we were forced to come to a standstill.

"Is there another route?"

"By horseback, yep ... down by the sea." After some thought, he added, "Maybe we should return to the hotel livery."

"We'll miss the train," I objected.

"There's always another tomorrow." Sharp again stood in his stirrups and looked all around. "Damn it, where's Joseph?"

"We'll need to force the manager to give us rooms," I mumbled to myself.

"Never mind." Sharp said, "Goin' back will never work. That's why the sheriff was sittin' at the entrance to the hotel grounds. He wanted us to go back. He'll do the same tomorrow ... and I'm sure that son of a bitch has an ambush spot on the coastal horse trail as well."

"Then we forge ahead and hope he just sends us back ... or Joseph rides up to save the day."

"That's my thinkin'," Sharp said. "Joseph knows where they're gonna stop us. He thinks like an outlaw. That's why he ain't around here. He's close to that bend in the road."

"If we go forward, do you think we're riding into a shooting confrontation or a blockade?"

Sharp took a long moment to respond. "If he discovered we turned la Junta factions against him, he might meet us with guns blazin'. If he remains ignorant, his lust for money should harness him."

"He knows," I said dejected. "Otherwise he would have quietly killed the coolies on the fishing boat. He went the way he did to teach the tong a lesson."

"I think yer right," Sharp said. "Let's proceed with our guns at the ready."

I nodded, then yelled into the stage. "We're going to the train station. Expect trouble. Keep your rifle barrels sticking out the windows. If we get stopped, don't start shooting. They'll probably just send us back. While we're talking, pick yourself out a target. Just in case."

"No!" William exclaimed with a cracking voice. "These are criminals. I know these men. I've been their captive. They're tough, hard criminals. They know how to shoot … and they have badges. There's no way we can beat them. We need to return to the hotel. Now!"

I dismounted my horse, and in a single motion, lifted myself to the outside of the stage by stuffing my boot toe into a carriage step while holding the windowsill. I stuck my head through the window of the slow-moving coach to reassure William, when Jenny leaned around Jeffie and slapped William so hard, his head bounced against the door frame.

With her broken jaw, Jenny couldn't talk, so Virginia yelled, "Damn it, Will, shut up! You'll get us all killed, including my child. These men know how to handle their kind. I've watched them for years. Do what they say, or I'll shoot you myself."

"Yes … or we're done," Jenny mumbled.

William rubbed his cheek and appeared befuddled. "Divorce? Are you talking divorce?"

I could barely hear Jenny answer. "Not if you get me killed."

"I'm trying to save our lives," he protested.

"This is the West," Virginia said. "You can't cry your way out of trouble. Be a man and protect your wife this time."

"What? She caused that," William said. "She went berserk. Everything would have been fine if she had shown a little cooperation."

"Cooperation? They were going to rape—"

"You don't know that. They were trying to frighten us. Trying to—"

"We do know that!" Virginia said. "You sniveling weasel, don't you—?"

"You know no such thing. Are you—?"

"William, out!" I yelled. "Sit up with the driver. Now!"

The driver pulled up, and William didn't hesitate to get out of the stage. When he awkwardly climbed into the seat beside the driver, he appeared frightened as hell. I would have preferred him angry. I had to separate them, or one of the women might actually kill him. Perhaps my mother could settle Virginia and Jenny as we made our way toward the train station.

Sharp rode up alongside the driver. After a brief chat that I couldn't hear, Sharp nodded in my direction to let me know that the teamster would still drive us to the station. Then Sharp rode around the back and pulled up next to William.

"Listen, partner," he said, "don't aim that gun at anyone unless shootin' starts. Keep it pointed at the sky. They'll probably send us back to the hotel, an' we don't need someone on the other side gettin' all nervous 'cuz they have a shotgun pointed at 'em. Understand?"

"Yes." William looked up the road. "Do you think there's going to be shooting?"

"Relax, Will," Sharp said. "We don't know each other well, but ya seem like a good lad. Steve an' I have been in this type of situation too many times to remember. It's best to avoid 'em, but if ya can't, then I believe ya should try to talk yer way out. If that don't work, ya gotta fight. It's all right to be scared, but it ain't all right to turn into a wooden Indian like ya did back at that hotel. Square yer shoulders an' tell yerself ya ain't gonna lose this fight. Heard ya were a footballer. Ya win a fight the same way ya win at football. In yer head. Understand?"

"Yes, sure ... but the stakes are so much higher in a gunfight."

Sharp laughed. "Yep, they are, but how ya win's the same. Have a plan, keep alert, an' keep yer head about ya. Ya lose if ya act reckless, or ya don't act at all. Now relax. Ya'll do just fine."

Sharp rode away without giving William a chance to respond. As he headed around the back of the coach to take up his position, he whispered to me, "That boy could get us all killed."

Chapter 32

Once we were back in position, the teamster flicked his whip in the air, and the horses proceeded down the road, delivering us to our destiny. I could see no sign of the sheriff, but I knew he lay ahead of us. I was more scared than I had ever been before. I passed a hand across my wounded belly. I had had several fights since wandering out West and had survived them all unscathed. Until now. I suddenly feared my luck had run out.

Another factor rattled my nerves. I had fought once before alongside Virginia, in New York City of all places. She had been enormously brave and unflinching in the fight. I only wished William had half her courage or half of Jenny's rage, for that matter. Although I trusted my wife's judgment in battle, I didn't want her involved. It gave me something to worry about when I needed a clear mind. But it was worse than that. I was now a family man, with my son in the stage. If this went bad, it would put him and his mother in danger.

If possible, I vowed to talk, buy, or bluff my way out of this predicament.

The road ahead appeared empty. The coach driver moved at a dawdling pace, but I was tempted to order him to slow even further. That made no sense. The confrontation would come, no matter what. Better sooner than later. I could rely on Sharp, and I had faith that McAllen would show up to bolster our forces. My mother could shoot the eyes out of a charging wild pig, and Virginia had developed a reasonably steady hand with a rifle. Nora and William could make a lot of noise, possibly distracting the sheriff's men.

I saw the bend in the road that Sharp had mentioned. I cleared my mind. Most probably, trouble lay around that corner, and I needed to concentrate.

Sharp galloped up a bit and signaled me to follow. We both spurred our horses and sprinted ahead of the stagecoach. As we came within sight of the road beyond the curve, our fears became reality. Sharp held up his hand, instructing the driver to pull up. A two-foot wide tree trunk barred passage, and the sheriff and his men sat casually in their saddles just beyond it. I glanced at Sharp, and he signaled that we should proceed. I lightly flicked the reins against my horse's neck, and he moved forward in a slow walk.

Sharp and I already had our rifles unsheathed but kept them pointed skyward, the butts against our thighs. The sheriff didn't seem like he was ready to kill us, but looks can be deceiving. That thought caused me to assess my own expression, and I relaxed my jaw. I told myself not to be nervous but to remain ready.

The coach had stopped before the bend. I liked Sharp's strategy. With our families around the corner, if a gunfight ensued, they would not be in the path of bullets.

I signaled for Sharp to stop.

I judged we were still out of earshot but whispered just the same. "What will the deputies do if we kill the sheriff?"

"Try to kill us," he answered.

"Yes, I know, but after they overwhelm us, what will they do?"

"Will they attack our people around the bend?" He rubbed his jaw. "Steve, we have to assume they will. So … we gotta whittle down their numbers enough so the women can fight 'em off. That's my plan, anyway."

"I have a better plan. If shooting starts, we kill the lot of them."

Sharp nodded. Then he gave me a grin. "You kill the sheriff; I'll start with the man on the far left an' work my way to the center. After you kill the sheriff, shoot the man to the far right an' work your way to the center."

"You see something?" I asked.

"Just a hunch. The men on the outside appear more capable. Smart play if he put them out on the fringe."

"Okay, hope you're right."

"Come on in, gentlemen," the sheriff barked. "We won't bite."

"Stay a moment," Sharp whispered. "Maybe we can make him edgy."

"Your strategy assumes McAllen won't come to the rescue."

"In a fight, always assume the worst."

"The worst being?"

"The sheriff already killed McAllen an' sent the Pinks packin'."

"How? They're in my employ."

"Steve, there's a problem relying on Pinks. Their livelihood depends on the cooperation of the law, an' in this instance, we're fightin' the law." Sharp turned in his saddle. "Did you wire Joseph that these outlaws wore badges?"

"No. I kept it brief."

"That's what I was afraid of. Steve, we got to proceed on the assumption that even if Joseph's out there, he doesn't have confidence in his team. Pinks don't shoot at lawmen. Bad for business."

"Damn, you're right. I should have thought of that."

"Well, maybe the sheriff isn't a complete son of a bitch."

"You don't believe that, and neither do I. Think he's rattled yet?"

"Nope. He ain't shouted out again. He figured out our game, I 'xpect." Sharp examined the surroundings, which were lightly wooded with no structures in sight. No place for McAllen to hide. When he turned his eyes forward again, he said, "Let's go see what the sheriff has in mind for us."

We nudged our horses forward. I counted only eight men opposing us. Knowing the sheriff, all of them were capable gun hands. If it remained two against eight, there was only one way this could end. I started to swipe my hand across my belly but stopped before completing the gesture. I shouldn't remind myself that my skin could be broken by a bullet. I concentrated on the men on the other side of the downed tree.

When we pulled up short of the tree, neither of us said a word. We sat in our saddles, trying to look like we weren't intimidated. I suspected our confidence meant little to the sheriff.

He tipped his hat to Sharp and me.

The sheriff spoke. "I wondered what had happened to my favorite guests in our little town."

Sharp and I sat still, not reacting. One errant move would have initiated gunshots, and a lot of people would die. I sensed danger.

Then I heard danger. The coach came roaring up behind us. Damn.

I disciplined myself to not look around. I kept an eye on the sheriff, but his eyes were focused over my head as he watched the coach approach.

"If you'd be so kind," I said, "would you have your men haul that tree out of our way? We have a train to catch."

"Tree removal is not one of the duties of a sheriff. I'll notify the mayor when I get back to town. He'll have a crew out here tomorrow."

The coach had pulled up behind us, and I heard my mother snarl, "Move that tree, or I'll blast the lot of you to kingdom come."

"You sound mean, but do you know how to use that rifle?"

I took a quick glance back, and my mother was riding shotgun. William was nowhere to be seen. I quickly returned my attention to the sheriff, stifling any thought of what might have transpired to put her in charge.

The sheriff chuckled. "Hiding behind skirts, are we? Well, no need for alarm. This road should be clear by tomorrow. Take tomorrow's afternoon train, assuming there are no other obstructions in your path."

"Mister," my mother barked, "we are going to meet today's train. If you don't lift that tree out of our way, we will."

"I don't see how that's possible." He pulled out his watch and tapped it. "Even if that tree is hauled out of the way, it's too late. Even with a clear road, I doubt you can make it."

I pulled out my own watch, and after a glance, said, "He's right. The train leaves in fifteen minutes. We can't make it."

"It could be late," my mother objected.

"Our trains are never late," the sheriff said with a self-satisfied smirk. "But thank you for coming out of your hidey hole. Nice to know where my guests are." He tipped his hat to my mother. "And Mrs. Dancy, special thanks to you. If you hadn't sent mounds of luggage to the train station, I might have missed that you were skedaddling."

It appeared that the sheriff was going to allow us to return to the hotel. That bode well for our survival for this day. I thought through the options, keeping my attention fixed on the sheriff. Did he mean what he implied, or was he coaxing us to relax so our vigilance would waver? Would the manager give us rooms? Would the situation change tomorrow? Where was McAllen?

Then I heard my mother speak. "Unfortunately, our sojourn in your fine city has drawn to a close. I left you a letter about the arrangements for that other matter. It's probably in your office by now."

"Shut up, granny." The sheriff spoke harshly. "No one leaves until the money is handed over. No one."

"Then we'll return to the Del Monte," I said nonchalantly.

The sheriff bristled. "Not so fast. Someone needs to pay for killing my men in the hotel … and for this disobedience."

My attention became razor-sharp. No one spoke on our side. What did the sheriff have in mind?

He pointed at Virginia, who leaned out of the coach with her rifle pointed up, but at the ready. "Send her over. Have her walk." He waved his arm. "Around the tree. She's going with us."

"That's not happening," I said, tilting my rifle barrel slightly down.

Sharp added, "If ya attempt to take any of our party, we'll kill ya all."

The sheriff's fierce eyes shifted from me to Sharp. "You better think again, mister. There's eight of us."

"I got fourteen rounds. Plenty. I'll shoot ya twice."

"You son-of-a-bitch." The sheriff looked at me. "Tell your man to be careful. I don't need your money that bad. Rile me further and I'll kill the bunch of you where you stand."

Sharp leaned forward in his saddle. "Perhaps ya oughta take a peek behind ya before ya start shootin'."

I risked a glance to see what Sharp was referring to. I brought my eyes back to the sheriff in a flash. If the sheriff acted, I didn't want my attention distracted. I hoped my face didn't reveal the relief I felt. Then I realized that was exactly what I should show. Sharp was not bluffing, and showing relief on my face might convince the sheriff that the threat behind him was real.

Without breaking eye content with me, the sheriff asked one of his men, "Brad, anyone behind us?"

That was a savvy move. The sheriff had not survived this long in his dual lines of employment by being fooled into diverting his attention.

Brad said, "Five … six men. Heavily armed … and lookin' mean as rabid dogs."

The sheriff risked a quick peek and then swung back to glare at me. "You got a telegram out of here."

It was an accusation. "I did. Those men are Pinkertons, and they're in my employ."

I could see the sheriff's mind working furiously. The odds were about even, but we already had our guns at the ready, and if shooting erupted, he and his men would be in the cross fire. He knew retreat was not simple. We might not relinquish our edge. He'd remember that I let him walk away the last time the odds had been even. He'd conclude I would do the same again. I didn't want this to drag on, but I couldn't just shoot these men down. My family was right behind me. My wife held a gun, making her a target. And they were lawmen, which meant the Pinkertons might not help, especially if we shot first. They'd protect us, but they wouldn't murder for us. I needed a provocation, or this would be just another in a long line of unresolved standoffs.

My mother spoke. "Francis, maybe you'd better retire. With the trouble at the docks, it's already been a long day."

At the sound of his name, I thought the sheriff might have a seizure. His body tensed, his face turned red, and his lips tightened into a thin straight line. For a moment, I thought he would go for his gun. No such luck. Suddenly, he relaxed in the saddle and chuckled.

"Our business will be settled at a later date." He looked at me and then at Sharp. "Neither of you may leave town. I am hereby notifying you that you are subjects of an inquest and must stay inside the town boundaries until you hear otherwise."

"An inquest? For what?" I asked.

"The shooting at the Del Monte … and another gunfight outside of town. I have reason to believe the two of you were involved." He turned in his saddle and addressed the Pinkertons in a loud voice. "I am the legally elected sheriff of Monterey County. Your permission to work in California depends on your obeying the commands of local law enforcement. Do not interfere with my investigation, or I'll slap you with a restraining order that will create howls in your San Francisco and Chicago offices." He paused. "Am I clear?"

One of the Pinkertons responded, "Absolutely, Sheriff."

He smiled at me. "Your women, of course, are free to go. This time. But one of these women assaulted men who had been deputized by me. Unless you cooperate, Mr. Dancy, she will need to pay for her crime. That, of course, could be entertaining for us all."

He laughed and rode off.

After the sheriff and his men departed, our saviors walked their horses up to us.

"Cuttin' it a bit close, ain't ya, Joseph?" Sharp said.

Joseph McAllen kept a stoic expression as he dismounted.

"Taught to arrive in the nick of time," he retorted. "Saves the client money."

Chapter 33

Before we could celebrate our good fortune, Sharp said, "Let's get that coach turned around and get outta here. The sheriff rode off in the direction of Santa Cruz. He might come back any time."

McAllen hurriedly sent two of his team ahead to scout the way back to Monterey. The others created a protective ring around us as the teamster nudged the coach backward until he could change directions at the bend. As soon as we were on our way, Sharp and I took up positions on either side of the coach to protect our flanks. McAllen sent two Pinkertons to ride in front, and he remained in back with another man to guard our rear.

After we could clearly see an expanse of road in either direction, I dropped back alongside McAllen.

"Great to see you again. Really great. Sorry it's under these circumstances."

He smiled, closed-mouth. "Steve, you got a proclivity for trouble."

"Been peaceful until I decided to take a vacation."

"Yep, vacations can kill you."

"I apologize for pulling you away from your work. Hope all is well at the ranch."

"Yep. Making bushels of money. Not in your class, but I'm comfortable."

It had been a few years since I'd left his ranch to honeymoon in San Diego. A lot had probably changed, so I asked, "Any women in your life?"

He nodded. "Got a woman livin' with me now."

That surprised me. McAllen claimed he still loved his former wife. Had he found another woman to take his mind off her? It made sense, because honor would never allow him to harm her relationship with her new husband, especially since he was the town pastor and a good stepfather to McAllen's daughter.

"Anyone I know?" I asked, knowing he probably wouldn't tell me.

"Maggie," Sharp said as he sidled up alongside us, chuckling. "I'll save ya the embarrassment. He probably woulda strung ya along for a mile or two."

"More," McAllen deadpanned.

Maggie was McAllen's daughter and the reason he built his ranch outside of Durango. Sharp and I had met Maggie when she had been abducted at age fifteen, but now she must be a young woman in her early twenties.

"All the time?" I asked.

"Yep. She's my foreman. Damn good one too. Knows horses and men. Keeps 'em both in line. Fine at barterin' as well. Next year, she's gonna sell the herd."

"By herself?" I asked, incredulous.

As far as I knew, McAllen still sold his horses to the army and Pinkerton's National Detective Agency. Two male-dominated organizations. He had always been protective of his daughter, so letting her go without him to market horses seemed out of character.

"She's a grown woman. Don't need me at her side."

He didn't elaborate, and I didn't pry. Instead, I looked up the road to see the entrance to the Hotel Del Monte grounds. Then I wondered where we were going. We had no rooms.

"Jeff, would you and Joseph protect my family while I ride ahead and have a discussion with Mr. Nelson? Knowing my mother, she'll want to go directly to her room to freshen up after our aborted outing."

"Get us all rooms," Sharp responded, "an' don't forget the Pinkertons."

I tapped my heels against the side of the horse and galloped ahead. What argument would convince Nelson to give us rooms? For obvious reasons, he didn't like gunfights inside his genteel establishment. Couldn't blame him. I didn't like them either. I decided that I'd tell him the truth. The sheriff wouldn't let us leave town, so he couldn't get in trouble for boarding us. Plus, nothing more should happen until I handed over the money.

I pulled up to the livery in the rear, and a stable hand immediately came to care for the horse. When I entered through the guest door at the rear of the main building, I spotted Nelson racing toward me. His hotel information network worked effectively.

He approached with palms out and a worried expression.

I said, "Mr. Nelson, we need to go to your office."

"No, no, no." He made a flicking motion with his fingers. "Out. Out. I can't have you in my hotel. My guests are outraged."

I suddenly became angry. "They're going to be more outraged when they see the scene I'm about to make. You let murderers into your hotel. You allowed them onto the second floor. My family was endangered because of your negligence. They beat up a woman in our party. Do you want me to yell out what they threatened to do to my wife? Do you—?"

"No, no, you're perfectly correct. Let's go to my office."

When Nelson closed the door to his office, he spun toward me and threw his hands on his hips. "You have already caused me far too much anguish. Those men were deputized, and for all I know, on sheriff's business. You killed officers of the law, scared the hell out of my guests, endangered my daughter, and rode out of here like you were going to war. Despite your making a shamble of my business, I was gracious enough to have your injury cared for by one of my employees. Now … what the hell brought you back here? I thought you were on your way to San Francisco."

I spoke evenly. "The sheriff blocked the road and ordered us to return. We had no choice. I understand our altercation caused you problems, but think about what it has caused us. We paid a lot of money to ransom one of our party, my friend and I were ambushed on El Camino Real, a young woman was beaten severely because she wouldn't consent to rape, and my mother has nearly suffered a stroke with all this stress."

Nelson plopped into his office chair and ran his fingers through his hair. "I believe all but the last part. Forgive me, I don't mean to offend, but your mother gives other people stress; it doesn't afflict her. That woman might be a match for the sheriff and all of his men."

He was right, but I wondered how he had come to that determination. Then I knew.

"My mother forced you to hide our family and get Jenny and me medical attention, didn't she?"

"She did. She's a forceful woman."

"Bully for her. Now we need your hospitality again. You won't get in trouble with the sheriff, because he sent us here, and you won't have any trouble with us unless he sends brutes to attack our women again. We need the same number of rooms plus another suite for a friend who has arrived. My friend brought five Pinkertons, so we'll need appropriate accommodations for them as well." When he didn't respond, I added, "Again, I would like to remind you that your property will become useless if the sheriff continues to have his way in this town. We are your only chance of salvaging your investment. With my Pinkerton team arrival, we can win."

"I can't have you in the hotel. But I—"

"I'm sorry, but you will," I interrupted. "We have nowhere else to go, and remember, we have won every fight with the sheriff's men. They may be ruthless, but we're skilled and determined. You don't want to be on our bad side."

"Please, let me finish. I have a cottage out back. More like a house. It's in the woods and available. Please stay away from the main building. I can have food and beverages brought to you. No other guests need to know you're there. In a few days, when guests turn over, you may use the dining room. Will that work?"

"How many bedrooms?"

"Three. But I can have beds brought out and put on the veranda."

"How many?"

"As many as you need. The veranda wraps around three sides of the cottage."

I thought about it. Having McAllen and his men on our periphery might be an advantage, but we needed four bedrooms. One for my mother, one for Jeff and Nora, one for William and Jenny, and another for Virginia and me. With a couple bedrolls, we could squeeze Jeffie and Juanita into our room.

"Indoor plumbing?" I asked.

Nelson shook his head. "Only in the main building, but I can have the chamber pots emptied and washed daily."

"Morning and evening," I said.

"Okay, but the price will go up for extra services."

It irritated me that his first concern was profit, but after he told me the price, I realized that the cottage was cheaper than four suites plus rooms for the Pinkertons.

"Let's see it," I said.

We marched out the back of the main building, with Nelson constantly swivel-necking to see if anyone noticed us. I saw only livery hands. Guest who enjoyed the outdoors congregated on the front lawn, which provided an expansive view of the Pacific Ocean.

We continued along a pathway that led to a line of trees about fifty yards beyond the stables. After a few yards, we came to a pleasant meadow with a white cottage surrounded by flower gardens.

"This accommodation is for families … or the very rich or powerful who want privacy. Look inside. You have a lot of people, but I think we can make you comfortable."

As promised, the enclosed veranda circled three sides of the cottage. The rooms were small, but well appointed. The dining room table could accommodate ten people. There were nine adults in our party, plus Jeffie. The Pinkertons could eat outside. An alcove off the living room had been set up as an office and reading area. Nelson said he could have the furniture exchanged for a bed so it could serve as a fourth bedroom.

I walked outside and surveyed the immediate grounds. The surroundings had been cleared for about thirty yards, and pathways meandered through low-lying flower gardens. I examined the back of the cottage where there was no porch. A thick forest prevented me from seeing beyond the clearing.

"What's out there?" I asked.

"Hotel property," Nelson answered. "Just forest until the main road. About a half mile of wilderness. There's a path. A great place for a solitary walk when it's calm."

"Sounds more like a great way to sneak up on us."

Nelson's lack of response confirmed my fear. Oh well, we had enough Pinkertons to post a couple of guards at the rear. Plus, I didn't anticipate trouble from the sheriff until he got my money, or until we tried to escape again.

"Okay, Mr. Nelson. We'll take it. Get a bed in the alcove, two bedrolls for those who will sleep on the floor, and four beds or cots on the porch—two to either side. Since some Pinkertons will always be on guard duty, they can share beds. Also, have someone haul our gear in the stagecoach to the cottage. As soon as possible, have supper for fourteen delivered, along with four bottles of your best whiskey and a case of cold beer."

"Of course. Anything else?"

"If you can manage it, would you also bring the sheriff's head on a platter?"

Chapter 34

The sleeping arrangements were settled quickly because Sharp and Nora volunteered to sleep in the alcove. McAllen would sleep on the porch with the off-duty Pinkertons. In a little over an hour, we all sat at the dining room table, eating roasted turkey and fresh vegetables and drinking superb French wines. The hotel service remained excellent, despite the cottage being a couple of hundred yards away from the main building. Having escaped yet another life-threatening encounter, everyone was in a cheerful mood.

It was almost as if we were truly on holiday. That came to an end when Nelson came to supervise the cleanup by his staff.

After the dishes were cleared and the servants gone, Nelson nervously said, "The sheriff dropped by and insisted on knowing where I had boarded you."

"Did ya tell 'im?" Sharp asked.

"I had no choice."

"So he knows we're isolated out here in the woods," my mother said testily.

"Everybody relax," I said. "He knew we were on the grounds. He's just keeping track of us. If he wanted us dead, we would have been killed on the road."

"We need a plan," McAllen said. He gave the Del Monte manager a hard stare. "Please excuse us, Mr. Nelson."

No one said another word, but McAllen continued to glare at the hotel manager until he blinked and prepared to leave the cottage.

At the door, he added, "I'm leaving Jamie at your beck and call. Ring the bell hanging on the porch if you need anything. He'll come right over."

The door barely made a noise as he departed.

"Now what?" Mother asked.

"We plot," McAllen said.

"I thought you had a plan," she said.

"If I had a plan, I wouldn't have said we need a plan. Now, Steve, talk."

I was flattered. When we'd first met, McAllen would never have asked my opinion. He considered me a greenhorn … and a dandified city-dwelling greenhorn, at that. Worse, when I engaged his Pinkerton services the first time, I hatched a plan on my own and kept it secret from him. A mortal sin, in McAllen's mind. He believed that a client who didn't trust him was likewise untrustworthy. I glanced at William. No, I had never been that bad. By the time I had met McAllen, I'd already been in a gunfight in which I had killed two despicable, ne'er-do-well rapists.

McAllen was almost always right … and he was right in this situation as well. I had a plan.

I started talking. "The sheriff will murder us after we pay, so there's no reason to pay. But we can't stall much longer."

"A fight postponed is half lost already," McAllen said.

I nodded agreement. "We need to force the fight on our terms … and quickly."

"No, no, that's all wrong," William blurted. "Steve, you've got nothing but money. Pay the man. You're wrong. He would never kill us all. That's unheard of. There are nine of us now, plus we have Pinkerton protection."

"He will," I said. "He knows my background and my friends." I nodded toward Sharp and McAllen. "He's taken their measure. His so-called retirement depends on not leaving anyone behind with enough spine to hunt him down. Especially if they have the wherewithal. Which, as you pointed out, we do." I turned to McAllen. "I think he may fake a tong massacre. That'll put state and local law on the tong so heavy, they'll never pose a threat to him. He'll leave the Pinkertons alone, but the rest of us are doomed."

"I don't believe you," William said.

Jenny slapped the table. "No one cares what you believe." She spoke through lips so swollen, her words were hard to understand. "Please shut up."

I wanted to change the subject, so I asked McAllen, "Will the Pinkertons fight lawmen?"

"They'll protect this cottage and the people in it, but they won't attack a duly elected sheriff or his deputies," McAllen answered tersely.

I shifted in my seat. "That's what I thought. Listen, deputies will be watching us, and Pinkertons will guard us. They'll probably be within sight of each other. I want the Pinks to cozy up to the sheriff's deputies. Joseph, can you have them sidle up to their counterparts and strike up friendly conversations? They'll all be outside the cottage together, so it should be easy."

"To what purpose?" McAllen asked.

"To find out how many there are. To discover where they're posted. Know their shifts. Make them feel unthreatened. When we take the next step in the plan, we need them relaxed and confident that the Pinkertons do not pose a threat."

"Smart use of the team," McAllen said matter-of-factly.

"Next, we need to get the sheriff as isolated as possible. I don't want shooting. Too bloody, and the odds would be against us. No matter how well we do, some of us would die."

I let that sink in.

I couldn't assume they would put their lives on the line for me. I had to ask for their help. "Jeff ... Joseph ... will you fight with me again?"

Both nodded.

"You don't need me?" William interjected.

"No," McAllen answered abruptly.

William's face immediately showed relief.

"I want to help," Mother said.

"Me too," Virginia chimed in.

Before Jenny could form words with her broken mouth, McAllen raised the flat of his hand to quiet further comment. "Thank you, ladies, but whether we need your help or not depends."

"Depends on what?" Mother demanded.

"On the plan." McAllen sounded annoyed that he had to answer such a silly question.

Everyone looked at me.

Chapter 35

Good plans have well-defined goals. I explained that our goal was to kill the sheriff and leave Monterey without anyone following us to exact retribution. That meant killing any deputies who fought alongside him. To escape the consequences for killing lawmen, the fight had to be defensive, at the same time exposing the widespread corruption in the sheriff's office. To escape the consequences for killing la Junta members, we also had to make sure the tong and the Mexicans would harbor no ill will toward us.

With the goals in place, I told them my plan.

The first part dealt with safety of members of our party who had no role in the plan. I informed William that his task would be to protect Jeffie, Nora, Juanita, and Jenny. Instead of banking on William, I really intended to rely on secrecy for their protection. The five of them would be hidden where nobody could find them. I broached my idea and received concurrence on entrusting their safety to Carlos Hernández and hiding them in his village by the sea. If the worst happened, he could get them south to Los Angeles.

We needed a lure, one strong enough to get the sheriff away from other elements of la Junta Mixta. We also needed a landscape in which the sheriff felt safe, but we had an advantage. The lure was easy. Money. Lots and lots of money. We would need the entire two hundred and fifty thousand dollars to lure the sheriff into our trap. Risking the money was an easy decision, because I wouldn't hesitate to pay that much to protect my family. Besides, if my plan failed, money would be of no concern.

Sharp agreed to sneak away that very evening to visit Hernández. Because deputies undoubtedly watched the cabin and livery, he would go on foot. Luckily, the walking path behind the cottage led to El Camino Real. After reaching the highway, he would walk down the road until accosted by highwaymen. This would be a trial run for William and the others to use the path through the woods as an escape route. Sharp would arrange to have Hernández stage horses where the path intercepted the road, so when they reached the highway, they would be mounted.

Due to the tong's location by the wharfs, it would be impossible to go unnoticed to meet with them. Besides, Nelson had mentioned that the tong were in hiding until they received reinforcements from San Francisco or China. He had made this aside as he complained about his Chinese laborers failing to show up for work. Conveniently, the sheriff's raid on the tong ensured that they would not fight beside him. If we could free Max Lee, I believed we would have nothing to fear from the tong in the aftermath of our dealings with the sheriff.

After adjustments, we found roles for Mother and Virginia. In preparation for Sharp's secret mission with Hernández, McAllen stepped out to the back of the house and ordered his rear guard to search the walking path all the way to the highway. As Sharp changed into black clothing and boots, I had a whispered conversation with Jenny. I delicately told her that I was really entrusting my son's and Nora's lives to her hands. She had already guessed as much.

With group approval of the plan, the next step was a meeting with Nelson. I would also need to send telegrams finalizing the accumulation and transfer of cash for the extortion. Mother came with me.

As we walked to the main building, she said, "I don't like your plan."

"You didn't say anything in the cottage. What's the problem?"

"The odds aren't in our favor. I prefer plans that result in the annihilation of opponents."

"The sheriff will be dead."

"You don't even know that for sure." She walked on, and I sensed her foul mood. "Steve, one day, you'll meet your match. Someday, someone will be handier with a gun. Plus, you don't know what his ruffians will do after you kill the sheriff."

"I'm open to other ideas … or improvements in this plan."

"I know." She walked a couple paces before adding, "If I had any, I would have spoken up."

"I know that."

She laughed lightly.

We were approaching the hotel livery when she said, "Do you see that man watching by the tree?"

"I do. Wave. Friendly-like."

"Seriously?"

"Seriously, Mother. We're on the sheriff's business. Getting his money. No reason to make his men nervous."

We both waved. The man hesitated but finally returned our wave. We kept walking until we reached the rear entrance to the Hotel Del Monte. Nelson's office was toward the rear of the building. When neither his assistant nor daughter were about, we knocked lightly on his door. An irritated voice beckoned us to come in. We found Nelson behind his desk, looking forlorn.

"What's the matter?" my mother asked none too nicely.

"The sheriff just left. He made my options clear. I fear this will never end … or rather, when it does, it will end badly."

"Oh, quit bellyaching and act like a man," she responded.

"Everyone settle down," I ordered. "We're here to see you about putting an end to this. Soon."

"How?" he asked plaintively. "More shooting. More death." He put his hands over his ears, tilted his head down until it lightly banged the desk, then shook his head. "My god, this can't go on."

"Mother's right, quit bellyaching. You want this done with, then you need to arrange for the transfer of a large amount of cash."

He looked up hopefully. "You're ready to pay?"

"Almost. The money's in San Francisco. How do we get it safely to Monterey?"

He straightened up. "Not difficult. It's a larger amount than usual, but cash is transferred between here and there all the time by train and occasionally by stage."

"Why occasionally by stage?" I asked. "Trains seem safer."

"Strong boxes are sent from Santa Cruz and Monterey to San Francisco every day, and vice versa. Every train, every stagecoach. Most of the boxes are loaded with rocks. That way, highwaymen don't know when to rob us."

"Where in Monterey is the money delivered?" I asked.

"The bank, of course."

"Can you get it delivered here? To your office. I don't trust the bank. I want the money stored in your safe. Like we did with the ransom."

"Sure. Money usually leaves from here, but on occasion it comes in." He suddenly grew perplexed. "Why not the bank? Why don't you trust them?"

"If the sheriff can corrupt Western Union, he can get to anyone in this town." I indicated a photograph of his daughter on his desk. "As you know, he has different methods for different people."

Now Nelson appeared worried. "You know his hold over me, how he gets me to do his bidding, so why do you trust my safe over the banks?"

I shrugged. "Because you still know right from wrong. You push back when you can. You take some risks, and I appreciate how you've been open with me ... even when you've done me wrong as a result of the sheriff's orders."

"To my chagrin." He appeared to ponder the danger to him and his daughter. "Okay, what do you want me to do?"

As he spoke, he stole a glance at his daughter's picture. That gesture gave me pause. Nelson was an ally, but not a completely trustworthy one. I decided not to reveal his full part in this endeavor.

"I want you to have my quarter million dollars brought here to this hotel and put in your safe. I want you to count it before you store it away. Then tell the sheriff it's here and ready to transfer to him. Tell him I asked you to verify the count so you could assure him that the entire amount was ready. After I arrange the particulars for the handover to the sheriff, I want you to return my money to me." Then I lied. "That's your entire involvement."

"You want me to be an honest broker."

"We do." My mother spoke for the first time. "You're perfect for our purposes. To a reasonable degree, we trust you ... and the sheriff has a hammer over your head, so he trusts you as well. But, Mr. Nelson, let me assure you that if you abscond with our money, I have left instructions with my attorneys in New York to hunt you down to get it back with a pound of flesh. Literally. Taking that money will kill my family. I cannot abide that. It must go to the sheriff … otherwise … I'll take out my postmortem revenge on both you and your daughter." She leaned in close, keeping eye contact. "Have I made myself clear?"

Although we had arranged this gambit beforehand, her tone scared even me. Nelson just nodded vigorously. It was a shame to frighten the poor man further, but he would be suspicious if we just politely requested his help. Too much water under the bridge. My mother's theatrics ought to convince him that we seriously intended to pay the extortion.

"Mr. Nelson, we're not asking much," I said. "The sum is large, but the transaction is not anything you're unaccustomed to handling for your guests. Get the money here, count it, inform the sheriff, keep it safe, and deliver it to us so we can give it to the sheriff. Then we'll be out of your hair. Gladly, I might add."

"What about taking care of the sheriff, as we discussed previously?"

I shook my head vigorously. "No longer an option. He was an animal of Monterey County before we arrived, and he shall remain so after we leave." He appeared crestfallen. "I'm sorry."

"Are we in agreement?" Mother demanded, no sympathy in her voice.

"Yes," Nelson said.

He stood, extending his hand.

We shook perfunctorily and left his office.

When I complimented my mother's theatrics to McAllen, she blushed with the praise. That was a new one.

By the time we had returned to the cottage, it was dusk, and Sharp was gone. McAllen said that his men had encountered no surveillance at the back of the property, and Sharp had left while there was enough light for Hernández's men to recognize him.

Later, well after dark, the Pinkerton team leader reported. His men had shared cigarettes with deputies as an excuse to strike up a conversation. The deputies were standoffish, but not unpleasant. McAllen instructed the leader to not overdo it. They would have several days to evaluate their capabilities and intentions.

McAllen and I went out on the enclosed porch for cigars and whiskey. I had given up my pipe because it was a nuisance on the frontier but had picked up the habit of an occasional cigar in San Diego. Mexicans had an affinity for Cuban cigars, and it was considered impolite to decline a smoke when a business deal had been agreed upon. I found it a very civilized way to conduct business.

As we relaxed, McAllen and I went over the plan from start to finish. We made a few minor changes to help sell the story, but found it adequate, at least for our present circumstances.

"My guess is the day after tomorrow," I said at the end of our review.

McAllen pondered my comment. Finally, he nodded and asked, "Early evening?"

"I think so."

"Don't get fancy, Steve. Go straight at the son of a bitch."

I swallowed the last of my whiskey and stood to go to bed.

Chapter 36

Two days later, Sharp and I met with the sheriff to negotiate the money transfer. Nelson had already told him that we had the full amount on hand and that he was keeping it safe in his office vault. We were ready for the handover.

We met at a tavern close to the train station. The out-of-the-way location satisfied the sheriff's need for secrecy. Except that it was not so secret anymore. Sam and Rod kept a watchful eye on us from another table. From their seeming disinterest in our conversation, I surmised that the sheriff had told his most trusted deputies about his scheme. He'd probably understated the take but offered them enough to make it worth their while to disappear from Monterey, possibly even the state.

The sheriff insisted that Sharp take a seat at a third table. He wanted to talk alone with me. The watchers would need to decide if we or the opposing table were the subject of their interest. Sharp had it easy. He knew me well enough to keep his attention on Sam and Rod.

The sheriff started the conversation on a sour note. "I told you to have the money deposited in my San Francisco account."

"The money's the only leverage I have. It stays in my possession until I feel comfortable about the safety of my family."

The sheriff scowled. "Your mother and the others can leave by tomorrow's train, and you may have your stagecoach at the ready so you can depart immediately after the handover. We'll do the transfer at that rocky point with the cypress tree. Where you had the picnic."

"No, we won't," I answered. "Far too isolated." I nodded toward his deputies. "Your men could shoot us from a distance and throw us off that cliff into the sea, never to be seen again. Tomorrow is Sunday. We'll meet at noon outside San Carlos Cathedral. In the plaza across the street."

The sheriff laughed. "Smart. Just as services end. The church steps will be full of parishioners." He laughed some more. "Okay, Mr. Dancy, we'll meet in front of the devout Christians of Monterey."

He used his foot to kick over a tattered carpetbag. "Put the money in this bag. You may bring Mr. Sharp, but no one else. The Pinkertons must leave on this afternoon's train." I started to object, and the sheriff raised his hand. "No debate. The Pinkertons retire to San Francisco, or one of your family suffers. Severely. Probably your mother." He gave me a self-satisfied smile. "Besides, you and I both know the Pinks will never engage with legitimate lawmen." He thumbed his badge. When I didn't respond, he added an enticement. "You may keep McAllen around … but that's it."

"I could be in as much danger without the Pinkertons as with them," I mused.

Instead of getting angry, he smiled.

"I know you think this scheme has been a whim on my part, but I've been preparing for a fat mark for a long time. For example, I have an exceptionally good relationship with the San Francisco Pinkerton's office. As you'll learn in a moment, you're not the only one who can hire Pinks to do your bidding. I've also cultivated the Hip Sing tong in San Francisco. I've been the local law go-between for them for many years. It didn't take much for me to convince them that their brothers in Monterey have been cheating them. For a long time. Yesterday, the tong leaders were assassinated by their own brethren. The local tong is a shell. Just a bunch of illiterate coolies. Hip Sing will fill in the void in the next few months. Carlos Hernández, the aspiring don? He was easily bought, a simple-minded bandito with little ambition. He's set up well to control the county, and I don't fear him." He let me absorb that before adding, "Nor do I fear you and your friends." Another hesitation. "Don't worry, I'm not going to kill you."

His bluntness surprised me. "Why should I believe you?"

"Hey, I'm an honest man … most days." He laughed again, genuinely enjoying his little theatrics. "You suspect I'll murder your party after I get my money. You and your friends are the kind of men who could cause me trouble, but I won't kill any of you. Two reasons. First, there are too many of you. I considered a robbery gone bad, but you have too many hired guns for safety. I thought about burning down that cottage, but the three of us might not be able to keep you all inside. I thought about other scenarios, but they involved too many people, too many deaths, or too much risk. I don't need any of that." He reached inside his coat pocket and slid a legal document toward me. "I don't need you dead, because you're going to sign this." When I made no attempt to pick up the document, he added, "It makes Rod heir to your son's estate."

I looked over at his two deputies, truly perplexed. "What? Why?"

"A trust has been created for your son. In Rod's view, a substantial amount. If anything happens to me, Rod will receive a letter from my attorney informing him of his status as godfather to your son and heir. He's smart enough to figure out my revenge whether I'm in jail or the grave."

I thought a moment. "My son will have an accident."

"See, if you can figure it out, Rod can." He smiled. "So keep your friends in check or … well, or else."

He pulled something else from his pocket and handed it to me. It was two photographs, one of my home on Coronado Island and another of my mother's brownstone in New York City. I saw immediately that he had not been bluffing about engaging the Pinkerton's National Detective Agency.

"Don't think you can hide or get away," he said. "Just think of it as a business transaction gone bad. Like your investment in Edison products."

That pulled me up short. I had lost nearly a quarter million when I had liquidated my partnership with Sharp to sell Edison products in the western states. We had both married, and our priorities had changed. But how could the sheriff know how much that decision cost me? Again, Pinkertons. If he knew the amount of money I had lost and set the same figure for the extortion, then he had planned this in advance of our arrival, which meant he was getting information about future reservations from Nelson.

I had underestimated the sheriff.

But he wasn't done.

"You believe this is some elaborate retirement scheme, but it's not. I've milked as much as possible from this hick town. I'm moving to San

Francisco to continue my unscrupulous ways. I've secured a U.S. marshal appointment, and I've established connections with all the criminal elements in that fair city. And with local law and Pinkerton's. My operations will increase tenfold. I'm telling you this so you don't think I'll be easy picking up there. Sam and Rod will come with me, and I already have a gang of tougher men than the drifters around these parts." He laughed once more, probably at the expression on my face. "Bring the money tomorrow noon, then go on and live your nice little aristocratic life. Forget thoughts of revenge. They'll just get you and your family hurt. By the way, San Francisco is out of bounds for you. If I *ever* see you again, I'll kill you on the spot and send assassins to New York and San Diego."

I had guessed wrong about the sheriff. He had a far grander vision than I had ever anticipated. He hadn't mentioned it, but I was certain he also had city and state politicians in his pocket along with his appointment as a U.S. marshal, which meant federal connections as well. Then another thought struck me. Someone this prepared for an outlaw life probably knew more than a little about lethal fights.

"I can see you're thinking hard. Let me add another nugget for you to contemplate. I know about your history with guns. Pinkerton's has a large file on you. You're a deadly man. So are your cohorts. But I'm deadlier. I know all about you, but you know nothing about me. I fought supposed bad men all over the West before I came to Monterey. Not one stood a chance against me. I enjoy duels. I win duels. So don't get any fancy ideas." He smiled. "Your son needs a papa."

"What's your real name?" I asked.

"Clever, aren't you? That Francis story gave people something to gossip about. My real name is Frank Wilson. I'm telling you that so you'll know who you're dealing with."

I had heard about him. Supposedly the best gunman in Texas and points north. Or south, for that matter. How did he wind up here on the edge of the Pacific Ocean? Dumb question. The same way I did. But he was more than an experienced killer. He was smart. And he planned ahead.

He slid the legal document further toward me. "Sign it."

I did.

Chapter 37

To the extent possible, I had tried to relax that afternoon. My meeting with the sheriff had not gone as expected. I corrected myself. The sheriff now had a name: Frank Wilson, gunman extraordinaire. Ambitious, intelligent, and educated. I wondered about my plan. Would he see through it?

He would or he wouldn't. It didn't matter anymore. The die was cast, and now we had to be ready either way. I reconsidered everything. We were as ready as could be, considering the circumstances.

All of us in our party went about our business.

Virginia and Mother had played croquet on the front lawn and then went into the hotel for tea. McAllen saw his team off at the train station. Sharp kept an eye on our watchers. More than an eye. He chatted with each in turn. They may have thought he was trying to distract them, but he was really assessing their commitment to the sheriff's nefarious scheme. William stayed inside the cottage, keeping himself busy playing with Jeffie. He gave me a wide berth all day. I suspected he didn't want to be pulled into my plot at the last moment. Jenny continued to heal but still had difficulty talking. I left her alone to her brooding. Her relations with her husband seemed distant. I couldn't tell if it was because she was hurting, or if his weakness had offended her. The few times we crossed paths in the cottage, I saw fire in Jenny's eyes. I didn't know what she would do after her recovery, but I had witnessed her wrath in the past and was not anxious to see it again. I could only hope she would be satisfied with the retribution we had in mind.

Today was the day. Not tomorrow, outside the church. The time had come to act. The riskiest part of our plan was getting William, Nora, Jenny, Juanita, and Jeffie to El Camino Real during daylight. If Frank Wilson took the bait in the early evening, then these five had to be secured safely away well before he stumbled into our trap.

Before departing for the train station, McAllen's team had confirmed that the sheriff's men hadn't been watching the rear of the cottage. Sheriff Wilson had assumed that if he watched the livery, he'd know if we attempted another escape. Maybe he wasn't omnipotent. With the cash in Nelson's office vault, his extortion scheme was about to pay off. Maybe he had become careless. Soon, he would no longer care where we were or what we did.

I was on the front porch, pretending to read. I couldn't concentrate, so although I occasionally turned a page, I had no idea what the printed words had said.

McAllen climbed the three steps to the porch and walked over.

"It's time," he said evenly.

I stood and stretched. McAllen meant it was time to send William, Jenny, Nora, Juanita, and Jeffie to meet up with Hernández.

When I entered the cabin, I saw that someone had stacked two carpetbags by the back door. Good. They were traveling light.

William came out of his bedroom.

"Will, thank you," I said. "Do you have a pistol?"

"Jenny and I do. We'll get Nora and Jeffie to Los Angeles safely, don't worry."

"Los Angeles? Sounds like you assume we'll lose. We'll be fine, and so will you. We'll meet you at Hernández's place, and then all of us will go home in peace."

"Of course, of course. I didn't mean to imply that you wouldn't make it. But … I just wanted to let you know that if the worst happens, I'll get Jeffie to safety."

I masked my irritation. William had said Los Angeles, not San Diego. I bet he had already decided to dump my son with Nora and run east.

Carrying a Winchester, McAllen said, "I'll escort them to El Camino Real."

I nodded appreciation. I'd feel better once the four of them had been handed over to the Mexican bandit. Funny, I trusted Hernández more than William.

Jenny and Nora came out together, Nora leading Jeffie by the hand. I knelt down and hugged him goodbye and told him to be a good boy. Nora looked nervous, but Jenny appeared downright enraged. Her slurred words confirmed her demeanor.

"William, you carry both bags. McAllen, take the lead. I'll be the rear guard. With luck, some of those sons a bitches will try to stop us."

She held a pistol in each hand. I felt pity for anyone who gave chase.

When Sharp had met with Hernández, the negotiations had gone well. It helped that Hernández had received a letter from San Francisco lawyers, confirming that they were working with my mother's attorneys in New York to secure Carlos Hernández clear title to a large tract of land in California. It was further down the coast, but that didn't displease him. Carlos Hernández would officially become Don Carlos. As an added benefit, the demise of the sheriff would put Hernández's lieutenant in control of the entire county.

In less than an hour, McAllen returned to inform Sharp and me that our group had been escorted away by Hernández's men. It was time for me to change clothes and take my position in our drama. As I entered our bedroom to put on my tailored charcoal suit, I felt more nervous than expected. I examined my feelings. I didn't fear Sheriff Wilson's gun as much as I feared his intellect. If he saw through my plan, I would not see morning. Even if the sheriff won and got away with all the money, a cloud would perpetually hang over Virginia and my son. This had to work.

In a few minutes, I walked over to the main building. For all intents and purposes, I looked like a lawyer going to meet a client. As I traversed the path, I nodded at two deputies, one watching the cottage and the other keeping an eye on the livery. Neither worried me. If necessary, they would be handled when the time came.

Inside, I found Virginia and Mother at a corner table, taking afternoon tea. I sat down beside them and ordered tea for myself. As I munched on one of those silly little sandwiches, Virginia told me they had seen nothing unusual. I looked around. They had picked an out-of-the-way table in the main parlor for guests who wanted to watch more than to be seen. As my gaze shifted around the room, I saw the manager's office door. Perfect.

I don't like tea. When it arrived, I put so much cream in the dainty cup that it tasted like warm discolored milk. I occasionally sipped at it anyway. Virginia and Mother kept up a constant banter as I surveyed the lobby. I hoped I looked like a bored husband instead of a lookout. In about an hour, I was rewarded for my patience.

The sheriff sauntered into the Hotel Del Monte like he owned the place. He carried the type of black leather bag frequently used by doctors. Bracing him on either side, Sam and Rob looked purposeful. As casually as possible, I checked the back entrance. No additional deputies. Exactly as I had expected. Sheriff Wilson didn't want additional witnesses to what he was about to do.

The sheriff saw us but seemed unconcerned. We were dressed formally, taking tea, and engrossed in our own conversation. Mother stood to excuse herself. In a normal voice that still carried, she announced that she needed to return to the cottage for her arthritis medication. As she sauntered out, Virginia and I continued to talk animatedly.

The sheriff knocked and entered Nelson's office before he heard a reply. Sam and Rod sat down in wingback chairs positioned outside the hotel manager's office. When I glanced over, they pretended to ignore me.

In a few minutes, Sharp and McAllen entered using the rear door. They walked over to our table and chatted a moment, then greeted my mother as she returned. They turned as if to go to the bar but stopped midway when they apparently noticed Sam and Rob. They sauntered over to the duo like they didn't have a care in the world.

As they approached, Sharp said, "Hey, boys, glad I spotted ya. Yer man by the livery asked me to give you a message. He ain't feelin' so hot an' needs relief."

"Tough. Tell 'im to stay on post," Sam said.

Sharp answered, "I ain't yer errand boy. Tell 'em yerself."

Just as Sam was about to say something nasty, McAllen whipped out his Smith & Wesson .44 and bludgeoned Rod across the temple. Sam started to rise to better reach his pistol, when Sharp hit him with a roundhouse that put him back in the chair with a thud.

I scanned the lobby, but nobody had noticed. When I returned my gaze toward Nelson's door, Sam's and Rod's heads had been positioned against the chair wings to look like they were resting.

I walked over to the group of four men, two friends and two unconscious enemies.

"Sure you don't want company?" McAllen asked.

"No … but don't let Wilson leave that office alive."

McAllen nodded grimly. "Understood."

I tried the door handle. As anticipated, the office was locked. I pulled a key from my pocket and unlocked the door. I pulled my Colt and cocked the hammer.

I took a deep breath and quietly stepped into Nate Nelson's office.

Chapter 38

Nate Nelson was on his knees. Blood trickled from his nose, and his collar was disheveled, as if someone had wrenched him around by it. One hand reached inside the open office safe, while the other stuffed a bundle of bills into Wilson's black satchel. The sheriff had his gun pointed at Nelson.

Perfect timing.

"How'd you get in here?" Wilson asked, startled.

"When I entrusted my money to Mr. Nelson, I insisted on an office key so I could check on the safekeeping of my cash. What's going on?"

"I'm taking my money now."

"I thought we set the exchange for tomorrow at noon."

"I'm taking it now," he repeated. "No need to dally … or risk a double cross."

"You don't trust me," I said lightly.

"I trust you as much as you trust me. Now put that gun away and leave us to this."

"I'm afraid I can't." I watched Wilson's eyes narrow. "That's my money you're stealing from Mr. Nelson's safe."

I could see in his eyes that he immediately understood the implications. I had accidentally interrupted a robbery. He was a fast thinker … that didn't bode well.

Wilson slowly shifted his body in my direction, all the while keeping his gun pointed at the back of Nelson's head. "I presume it would be useless to call out for Sam or Rod."

"You would presume correctly."

"And my deputies on the grounds?"

"Less mindful than usual."

He considered his options. "This gun is cocked, and the trigger pulled so it's ready to fire at the slightest twitch. If you shoot, Mr. Nelson dies."

"I know."

I said nothing further.

"Well, we don't want Mr. Nelson's death on our conscience. Maybe we should both holster our weapons." He smiled. "What do you think, Mr. Nelson?"

Since I had entered the room, Nelson hadn't moved in the slightest. Now he appeared reluctant to even move his lips. Eventually, he said, "Good idea."

I waited a couple beats, then said, "Both together and both very slowly."

Wilson nodded but didn't move his gun.

I dropped my aim imperceptibly.

Wilson did the same.

We each gradually lowered our guns and slipped them back into their holsters.

Wilson let his hand rest beside his pistol. "It's just you and me. A duel. I like that."

"Don't be rude to Mr. Nelson. He's here too."

"We should allow him to leave. He might get hit by a stray bullet."

"No!" I said firmly. "Mr. Nelson, don't move a muscle. He's going to use you as a diversion or shield."

"Still no trust?" Wilson asked pleasantly.

"None."

He seemed perfectly relaxed. "I promise you a fair fight."

What was he up to? If he found a way, he would never give me a fair fight. He knew I was skilled with guns and had won several gunfights. He had a quick mind and wanted an edge. Hell, I wanted an edge.

"Will you allow Mr. Nelson to leave?" I asked.

"Yes. I won't use him to cheat."

I said, "Go."

"I don't know if I can move," Nelson said in a quavering voice.

"Nate, move away from the sheriff. Slowly. Very slowly."

He started to stand.

"Stop!" I yelled.

He held.

"Crawl. Stay low and crawl away."

Nelson crawled all the way to the office door. He turned that handle from his knees and crawled out. I had only wanted him to crawl until he got away from Wilson, because I suspected the sheriff wanted to slip behind or shove Nelson when he came within reach.

Wilson remained perfectly still, seemingly amused at my paranoia.

"I don't need tricks," Wilson said.

I didn't respond.

"I'll give you credit for foresight," Wilson said. "And trickery. You lured me into this office to commit a criminal act so you could justify shooting me. But tell me, how will you eliminate the threat against your son? If things go badly for me, Rod will seek his reward when he gets that letter from my attorney."

"I signed those documents as Steve Dancy. New York courts have an affidavit stating that if I use that name, I signed under duress. Your attorney has already been informed."

"Which attorney?" he said incredulous.

"Mathew Davidson in San Francisco." Now it was my turn to smile. "The document you had me sign was on his letterhead."

"You couldn't notice that … no, I don't believe you."

"There are precautions the extremely wealthy take when they venture into a raw frontier. I sign official documents Steven Gregory Dancy, not Steve Dancy. Reading letterheads at a glance comes from years of signing legal papers."

"Damn you. I planned this for years." He sounded frustrated. "Your trick won't work. My lawyer will find a way around your little affidavit."

"He won't. And … with his client dead, he won't even try."

He almost went for his gun. I saw it in his eyes, but he instantly recovered from his disappointment.

"No matter," he said lightly. "In a moment, I'll kill you and walk out with the money. Nothing's changed."

He said that to get an edge, but I had a better one.

"You might kill me, but when you walk out that door, Joseph McAllen will put a .44 through your heart. And Joseph always keeps his word."

A flicker of concern told me I had rattled him.

"I'll shoot your friends on the way out the door. Been in tougher spots."

I sensed that he wanted me to respond in anger. We were done talking. I kept my concentration totally on Frank Wilson.

His attention was fully on me.

We both held still as statues.

The world stood still … until it didn't.

Two shots rang out.

Both from my pistol.

I didn't think about pulling my gun. It just happened.

Wilson's startled expression turned into a grimace as he fired his weapon into the floor. Then his face went blank. Frank Wilson was dead standing up.

"You bastard," he said before falling.

Chapter 39

Through the closed door, I yelled, "Joseph, can you hear me?"

"Yes," came the clear response.

"Don't shoot me. I'm coming out."

"I'll try," McAllen answered.

I opened the door, but instead of seeing Joseph, I saw and felt Virginia make a running leap into my arms.

With tears rolling down her cheeks, she gave me several sloppy kisses. "That took forever," she said. "Thank God, you're safe."

I smiled. "Seemed like only moments to me."

She playfully slapped my shoulder, leaned back to look at me, and then kissed me again.

Sharp and McAllen came over. Their congratulations weren't as wet as Virginia's.

After handshakes and backslaps, I said to Joseph, "I'll try?"

"Good thing Virginia jumped in the way," McAllen responded. "You had me all worked up to shoot someone."

Sharp laughed before saying, "Joseph, I thought we told ya not to do humor. Ya do it wrong."

When we broke up, my mother came over, looking stern as a schoolmarm. She looked me up and down. "One day, the fight won't go in your favor, Son. I'm ordering you to stop this reckless gunfighting … right now. Do you hear me?"

"I do, Mother. And I love you too."

Chapter 40

The next morning, Mother and I met for breakfast. She would soon depart for the train station to travel back to New York. McAllen never wasted time; he was already riding for Colorado and his ranch. William and Jenny would leave Monterey on the same train as Mother but would switch to a Nevada line in San Francisco. Only Sharp and Nora weren't scattering to the winds. They would join us in San Diego for an unspecified spell. Before we all set off in different directions, I needed to discuss something with my mother.

"Okay, out with it," she said as she sat.

"Mother, you just arrived. Let's get coffee first."

"Fine. Order coffee, but as soon as you do, tell me what's on your mind. I don't want to be late for the train."

The train doesn't leave for three hours. We have time."

"You may have time, but I'll not stay a moment longer than necessary in this godforsaken village. I'll grant you it's pretty and the hotel adequate, but this holiday may put me off traveling until the end of my days. Which, by the way, may not be that much longer, so if you have something to say, say it."

"In a moment. First, a gift."

I handed her a one-hundred-dollar bill folded in quarters so that only Abraham Lincoln showed.

As she unfolded it, she said, "What's this? Currency with a hole in it."

"Keep it as a souvenir of your most memorable holiday."

"Memorable, yes, but not in a good way." She put her pinkie in the hole and twisted it around. "Good grief, that nasty sheriff shot your money." She refolded it and slid it into her bodice. "Better than shooting you, I suppose."

"I prefer it," I said. "His errant shot went into the money bag. Fitting."

"If you say so. Now what is so important that you're holding up my departure?"

I smiled at her flippancy but noticed she did not offer to return the bill.

I folded my hands in front of me and asked, "How would you improve this hotel?"

"What? Good gracious, Son, I said, get on with it."

"I am. What would you do to improve the Hotel Del Monte?"

With an irritated expression, she spoke at a breathtaking clip. "First, a better chef. The food is barely adequate and far too provincial. A more cosmopolitan menu. The hotel has a grand view, but I would have built it closer to the ocean. People who travel across the entire nation want to feel the sea, not just see it at a distance. The décor is affluent but boring. It should have been built and decorated in the Victorian style that's becoming the rage among the smarter set. Where's the entertainment? A person can't play lawn games all day and night. What they call a ballroom is tiny, dark, and uninviting. Offering dances only on the weekends is ridiculous. We're here for a holiday, after all. There should be a chamber orchestra every night … and maybe a harpist or violinist at supper. Did you see how some of the men dressed for supper? Outrageous. If you want to attract the very best people, you need a milieu that encourages people to dress properly."

She gave me an exasperated look before adding, "Now, have I sufficiently annoyed you? I was perfectly willing to leave without complaint, but you insisted."

"On the contrary, you've proved me right."

Now she looked puzzled. "You picked this hotel, and I just told you it was barely adequate. How did you conclude that you were right?"

I smiled. "Mother, I brought us all here because I'm considering a business investment. I wanted you to experience the best vacation hotel the West Coast has to offer. I totally agree with your assessment. Let me ask you, if this hotel had all of the characteristics you mentioned, would people travel from the East Coast for extended stays?"

The delivery of our coffee service gave her an excuse to think about my question. As the server departed, another guest came up to our table. With a flourish, Carlos Hernández waved his arm across his waist as he made an overly deep bow to Mother.

"Buenos días, Señora Dancy," Hernández said with an engaging smile. "I came to wish you a pleasant journey home."

Mother looked at me. "Who is this?" she demanded.

"Mother, may I present Carlos Hernández? You are working on his behalf with our New York attorneys. He was of great assistance in our recent difficulties."

She appraised the man. Hernández was dressed in a buff-colored suit tailored in the Spanish style. His hair was cut and neat, and he was clean shaven. Most impressive, he wore expensive boots made of snakeskin. In all, he looked dashing.

"I see." She held out her hand. Rather than shake it, Hernández kissed it. She continued, "We are all grateful for your assistance. To relieve you of asking an awkward question, I'll tell you that the legal matters are proceeding quite nicely, and you will soon be the leading landholder in San Luis Obispo County." She handed him an envelope. "Inside you will find the name and address of attorneys in New York and California who are handling the arrangements. Feel free to contact them to establish your own line of communication."

Hernández slipped the envelope into his inside coat pocket without examination. "Gracias, Señora. I appreciate your forthrightness."

"Where were you educated?" she asked.

"The Franciscans taught me."

"They apparently did a fine job." She assumed the expression she used to scold me. "Señor Hernández, you will soon have a hacienda befitting a don. I presume you also have money from your illicit affairs. You're educated. I suggest you reconsider your career. Live as an example to the rest of your people."

Instead of being insulted, Hernández appeared impressed. "I will do my best, Señora. I … uh …"

"No need to explain," she said. "If I were in your position and learned that someone who owed me something was leaving town, I would also verify the delivery of that obligation. But don't be concerned. Dancys always fulfill their obligations. In fact, I have secured the release of an individual in New York of interest to the local tong. I met my side of the bargain despite the unexpected demise of the tong elder I had dealt with."

"You and your son are to be commended on your honor."

Without waiting for a response, he bowed again and regally marched out of the dining room as if he were already the most important person in the state.

Without preamble, Mother asked, "Where do you plan to build this vacation hotel?"

"San Diego. How did you guess?"

"You're obvious, despite your meanderings around the subject. I knew you weren't going to buy this one, because many attributes I mentioned can't be added after the fact. The only alternative is to build. I just didn't know the locale. Is San Diego as picturesque as Monterey?"

That caught me by surprise. "Different. There is no rugged coastline with spectacular views ... but pristine white sand beaches extend for miles. Rocky cliffs are visible in the distance—part of the peninsula that protects a massive natural harbor. It's a much better venue for sailing or rowing ... sheltered or open sea. I believe it's truly unique."

She gave me a steady gaze. "Sounds as if you've already decided. Why do you want to discuss it with me?"

"I want you to participate. Not just in the financing, but in the design. You know what your social set expects when they travel." I paused. "I would like your help."

She reflected a moment before asking, "Do you own the property?"

"Yes, on an island, actually a peninsula in San Diego Bay. The hotel would be built right on a beautiful beach, where people can step out of their rooms for a sunbath or swim in either the ocean, a quiet bay, or a freshwater pool. My home is adjacent to the property. Right now, the island is mostly barren, but we're developing a plot plan for vacation homes and commercial areas. The city of San Diego is a ten-minute ferry ride across a protected band of water."

"I don't like the sound of this barrenness, and you may be underestimating the cost to build a proper vacation hotel. They are hugely expensive. People come for rest, unusual activities, and entertainment.

While playing or relaxing, they expect to be catered to in the fashion of royalty. They want to impress their friends and meet influential people." She smiled indulgently. "Stephen, dear, it's hard to attract the aristocracy. The surroundings must be breathtaking, the accommodations and service unparalleled. They won't come unless they know they'll meet people of equal caliber. And the venue must allow them to show off their clothing, jewelry, dancing skills, and whatever else they're proud of." She gave me a condescending smile. "Dear, you must offer them something that's unique but feels exactly like home. Do you understand?"

"Of course. I grew up in that scene. I hated it, but I understand it."

"Then why do you want to build the same scene again?"

"I've asked myself the same question. It's about more than making money, but I'm not just trying to relieve boredom. I want to build something big in this untamed land. Something permanent. Something people can marvel at a hundred years from now. Even longer."

"Do you have partners?"

"Of course. This is a big project, and I need people with the kind of connections that can get this thing going."

"Do you have a name?"

"Hotel del Coronado."

"That will never do—it's Spanish!"

"Mother, it's on the border with Mexico, and everything in San Diego has a Spanish flavor. Don't worry, the architecture will be Victorian, and the service and menu continental."

She sipped her coffee and then said, "I suppose we can emphasize the Spanish rather than the Mexican."

I swallowed my irritation at her prejudice. She was an elitist. That's why I had asked for her help. She could make sure the design attracted the powerful, and her financial participation would ensure that she would convince her social class to come out in droves. Whether I liked the snobbish rich or not, I needed them to make such a huge financial endeavor prosper. Otherwise, bankruptcy would forever loom over the enterprise. The Hotel del Coronado had become an obsession. I really wanted to build something grand. For that, I would have to put up with my mother's peccadillos.

When I didn't respond, she asked, "What do you want from me?"

"Whatever you are willing to invest, and I want you to review the design, both interior and exterior. When completed, I want your advice on service issues, recreation, entertainment, menus—"

"Enough, I get the picture. I'll invest the same amount as you, and I'll advise in the areas you mentioned. To tell the truth, I'm happy to see you've found challenging work that doesn't entail shooting nasty men before they shoot you. This is much more befitting your age and station."

I cringed slightly but simply said, "Thank you, Mother."

"Why did you look troubled when I said that?"

I took a sip of my coffee to stall. I decided she could read me too well to obfuscate.

"There are parties who do not want this to proceed. They are not New Yorkers, but they're capable people who have political backing and—"

"And guns," my mother said disgustedly.

"Yes."

"And that's why your partners pulled you into this deal."

"No, Mother. I wish that were true. Then I could just withdraw from the project. No one in San Diego knows about my background. I pulled in my partners, not the other way around."

"How do you intend to handle this?"

"Defuse the situation, bribe my own politicians, buy my opponents, hire Pinkertons ... anything to avoid violence."

She gave me a stern look. "And can you?"

"When I left San Diego for a peaceful holiday in Monterey, I believed I could." I threw up both hands. "Now, hell, how would I know?"

She tapped her fingers on the table. "Okay, I'm in ... We'll always be family, but in this affair, we're business partners. Do you know what that means?"

"Yes, Mother, I know what that means. I've seen you in business dealings. No one has crossed you and survived financially."

"Good. You understand." She folded her hands in front of her. "Now, I have one condition. No personal violence. None ... or I will consider it a breach of contract."

"What about self-defense?"

She stood, straightened her dress, and marched out of the dining room.

Chapter 1

Despite Rincon's reputation as the best surf spot along the Santa Barbara coast, other surfers gave Greg Evarts a wide berth. He didn't flaunt being a cop, but the locals knew his profession. The teens and young adults in the water were normally highly territorial, but they didn't want trouble with the local gendarmerie. Evarts purposely acted standoffish. He had no desire to compete or socialize with this younger crowd, but they'd be surprised to learn why. He wanted to avoid arresting them for beach misdemeanors or inland petty crimes. He knew what was going on. He had grown up on this same beach but had left behind his own minor delinquencies. Most of these kids would as well. He wanted to give them a break, but he didn't want to be taken advantage of because he was a fellow surfer. That would lead to sorrow—for them and for him.

Evarts seldom surfed in stormy weather. He didn't fear lightning. Electrical storms almost never accompanied rain in Southern California. Here, it drizzled, often for days. Nebraska might get an inch of rain in less than an hour, but clouds over the Golden State politely sprinkled moisture so sparingly that a full-inch accumulation could take days. No, Evarts didn't surf in the rain because he was getting old. Older, at any rate. He preferred to ignore having turned forty a couple of years before, but his aching joints reminded him daily. The young might surf during nasty weather, but Evarts preferred clear skies, no wind, and waves that didn't block out the entire sky.

None of these desirable elements were present today. The sideshore wind caused choppy water, heavy clouds hung low overhead, and the waves were thick and ranged from six to ten feet, with occasional sets more than twice his height. Bigger than Evarts preferred. He had gone in the water because he had given up waiting for a calm, sunny day. An endless line of storms had battered California, and ominous clouds had hung over Santa

Barbara for nearly three weeks. Inland areas of the state had become saturated with rainfall, but Santa Barbara had received only a constant drizzle that irritated locals addicted to sunshine.

Evarts examined the sky. He could discern not even a dull glow where the sun would be at this hour. He swiped water from his eyes. The rain was bad enough, but the wind made the ocean surface bumpy, and the nose of his board kept splashing salt water in his face as he paddled. He wanted to keep a clear eye out to sea, so it presented more than an annoyance. The larger, outside waves could be brutal, and he didn't want to be caught inside in what surfers called the impact zone. People generally thought of water as benign. It watered gardens, you could drink it, bathe with it, freeze it to chill a drink or a sore back, swim in it, or laze on the surface in a boat or on a floater. Water was an essential element of life, useful and often great fun. But surfers knew water could also be a killer. No one who had been hit by a huge wave disrespected moving water. You couldn't fight it. You couldn't beat it. You could only get out of the way or let it throw you around like a rag doll in a Rottweiler's grip.

He shook his head, scattering droplets of water in every direction. He was not having fun.

Evarts caught a head-high wave. After a bumpy, mediocre ride, he decided to call it a day.

No one yelled a greeting on the beach as he made the long trek to his vehicle. None of his aging surfing buddies felt desperate enough to challenge the cold for treacherous waves with little promise. Evarts cursed as he visualized them in their warm kitchens, sipping coffee, and reading the newspaper or computer screens. He used a metal manual key to unlock his Mercedes-Benz high-roof extended cargo van. Electronic keys didn't fare well in water. The interior of his van had been customized as a twenty-first-century surf wagon, possessing every convenience known to wealthy surfers. He slid his board into its dedicated slot and used the portable shower system while standing in the street behind the van. He then climbed into the back and closed the door to change out of his wet suit. Most surfers wrapped a towel around them and removed their suit in the open, but it wouldn't do for the chief of police to get arrested for indecent exposure on Pacific Coast Highway.

Evarts had money but didn't think of himself as rich. Habit, he supposed. He had grown up middle-class surrounded by rich people in this seaside town referred to as the American Riviera. When he had returned from military service and joined the local police force, he could only afford to live in the navy town of Oxnard, forty miles to the south. Everything had changed five years before. His best friend had been gruesomely murdered, and he discovered that Abe had bequeathed to him his Santa Barbara estate along with far more money than he would ever need to maintain it and pay property taxes. During the process of solving the murder, he had learned some hidden truths about his family and ended up marrying the woman who had helped him solve a related mystery with national implications. Evarts could hardly believe that he used to think he enjoyed living alone. Since marrying Patricia Baldwin, he had discovered that he hadn't been content, just ignorant. At the time, four years ago, he had been head of detectives but had since been promoted by the city council to chief of police. His life was good—and if the rain would go away for a few days, everything would be perfect.

He hated rain. The worst duty for a police officer was going to a car crash. The carnage unsettled even the most jaded officer, no matter how many accidents witnessed. Unfortunately, rain made accidents a frequent affair. Cars dripped imperceptible amounts of oil on the roads, and when it eventually rained in uber-dry Southern California, the oil seeped to the surface to make it slipperier than a surfboard without wax. As chief, he seldom went to crash scenes, but they took a toll on his force that required careful management.

Evarts lived high up a secluded canyon in the foothills of the Santa Ynez Mountains. To get there, he had to drive State Street through the main part of town, which the city advertised as the most beautiful downtown in America. Despite the exaggeration, the Spanish architecture, abundant sidewalk cafés, curio shops, fine restaurants, and countless coffeehouses exuded the charm and relaxed atmosphere of a Mediterranean coastal village. As he drove home, Evarts paid attention to happenings on the street. This was his hometown. His job was to keep it safe.

After leaving the city proper, Evarts drove into the foothills and followed a serpentine road to a gravel path in front of a wrought-iron gate.

He pushed a combination on the security box, and the gate opened. After passing through, he drove a quarter mile on a private road that extended toward the sea. His house had been built on the apex of an outcropping that overlooked the coastline for miles in either direction. The white stucco house, with its flat façade and red-tile roof, had been built in the hacienda tradition. The crushed rock driveway, minimalist landscaping, and unpretentious entrance gave an impression of ordinariness while disguising a rambling home of over eight thousand square feet.

The large square house surrounded a huge central courtyard. To take advantage of the expansive view of the Pacific coastline, the primary living quarters were located in a two-story section at the rear. Evarts could walk the perimeter indoors or cut through the exposed courtyard. The drizzle had turned to a light rain, so he walked the longer, indoor route. Passing through the kitchen, he grabbed a cold pork chop from the refrigerator, gnawing as he continued to the back of the house.

He found his wife on her cell phone, pacing the grand hall that spanned the rear of the hacienda as she talked. This was their favorite room. The prior owner had it built for charity events and it could easily accommodate a hundred people, with an additional hundred outside in good weather. In truth, being a police chief was more political than law enforcement, so he continued to host half a dozen charity events a year. Besides, the substantial sum his friend had left him, and his wife's even larger family inheritance meant that they could afford to entertain extravagantly and make substantial donations to the community and national organizations.

While Evarts was growing up, his parents had never joined any organizations, donated to any charities, or fought for any causes. Beyond not having the wherewithal, his parents were insular. But now, his position and good fortune required him to meet the expectations of a well-to-do community, no matter how much he disliked showy events that cost twice what the charity received. In truth, he would rather make a substantial donation than host a house full of snobs.

He admired his wife's athletic stride as she paced the room. She enjoyed lazing about on Saturdays and remained dressed in stylish flannel pajamas, a term he considered an oxymoron except when she wore them.

She made the prosaic night wear look perfectly normal in this ostentatious room. In fact, all clothing looked appropriate on her. Her casual good looks, short light-brown hair, and engaging smile went well with jeans or a designer dress, and her lively green eyes, even behind her ever-present glasses, drew everyone's attention.

He checked his watch, a Christmas gift from her. The black Mühle Glashütte titanium diving instrument had cost more than all his surfboards combined. It was almost ten o'clock in the morning. Surfing was a break-of-dawn sport that got him home with most of the day still ahead of him.

He swallowed a mouthful of pork chop and said, "Trish, who—"

Baldwin stopped him with a single uplifted finger. She could do that. In fact, she often gave instructions with one or two fingers.

Because of her renown as an author, historian, and speaker, she had kept her name after their marriage. They'd met during an investigation of a supposed trivial matter that had violently escalated into a dangerous race across the country to solve a century-old conspiracy. At first, he'd thought they couldn't be more different. She was a college professor, and he was a cop. She came from wealth. At sixteen, he had worked sweeping out a surfboard shop. She grew up on the Upper West Side of New York. He grew up on the beaches of Southern California. She attended Berkeley and Stanford. He went to a state college. Her nonfiction books always hit the *New York Times* bestseller lists. The only thing he had ever published was a letter to the editor in the local newspaper.

Baldwin said into the phone, "Mr. Gleason, I understand. I'll be in Sacramento first thing Tuesday morning." After a pause, she added, "Of course, sir. Thank you."

She tapped to end the call, turned off her phone, confirmed that it had gone dark, and then exclaimed, "Shit!"

"The lieutenant governor?" Evarts asked.

She lifted her eyeglasses slightly and let them fall back on her nose. "Yes, damn it. They're in a panic over this damn rain. Rain, for Pete's sake."

"I take it they want you up there Tuesday?"

"I wish," Baldwin answered. "The commission meets at 8:00 AM on Tuesday, meaning I leave noonish Monday, and they want me to bring a week's worth of clothes. Damn it, I have classes, committee meetings, office hours, and a speech in Los Angeles on Thursday night." She threw her phone onto the couch. "Damn, I wish I had never accepted the governor's appointment."

The governor of California had appointed Baldwin to the Seismic Safety Commission, and she had been on the advisory council for less than a year. As a history professor, Baldwin had consulted for years with the Office of Historic Preservation while teaching at the University of California at Los Angeles and at the University of California at Santa Barbara, where she had transferred after their marriage.

"I thought that commission dealt with earthquakes, tsunamis, and volcanoes."

"Some idiot evidently believes a few days of rain can trigger one of those. I don't need some volunteer work to destroy my career. This is stupid."

"It may hamper your career, but it won't ruin it. It's Saturday. This storm will probably pass before you sit down for your meeting. You'll be back in time to make your speech."

Baldwin was scheduled to give the keynote address at the Abraham Lincoln Historical Society's annual conference. Lincoln was her specialty, preservation of historic sites a hobby. Evarts felt a twinge of guilt. She had intended to turn down the appointment, but he had convinced her that it would take little of her time while helping him with state officials.

"What are you eating?" she asked.

He held up the chop by the bone. "Last night's leftovers. I need protein."

He ripped off a piece of meat with bared teeth like he was ravished, and she laughed at his antics.

"Don't we make the couple," she said. "You walk around chewing on a bone like a caveman, and I've been talking to the lieutenant governor in pajamas. I'm surprised they don't deport us back to Oxnard with the riffraff."

"We had fun there. Maybe I can buy back my old house."

"No, I'm good. Just frustrated that this stupid commission can jump up and disrupt my life." She smiled to show she wasn't entirely serious and added, "It's all your fault, you know. I wanted to decline the honor … if it can be called that."

"You'll be back soon. You know bureaucrats, always making a big thing out of nothing."

She walked over to a sofa table and picked up her coffee. She took a sip while staring out to sea. "Perhaps not this time. I heard fear in Paul's voice. They got seven inches of rain in the last week."

"Seven inches? Our drizzles haven't added up to squat." He thought about the implications. "Did he say if any dams were in jeopardy?"

"Yes." She didn't turn away from the murky, cloud-enshrouded ocean. "All of them."

Also by James D. Best

The Shopkeeper
Leadville
Murder at Thumb Butte
The Return
Jenny's Revenge
Crossing the Animas
The Shut Mouth Society
Deluge
Tempest at Dawn
Principled Action, Lessons from the Origins of the American Republic
The Digital Organization

To be notified when I have a new book, please join my mailing list by sending me a note at jimbest@jamesdbest.com.

You can also receive email updates from my blog at http://jamesdbest.blogspot.com by leaving your email address in the Follow by Email box. Thanks again

Made in the USA
Columbia, SC
29 June 2020